Charm and Perfection

Love Comes Again Book 3

LuAnn K. Edwards

All scripture is from the New International
Version.

ISBN: 978-1-952661-22-8

Dedication

This book is dedicated to my husband Kenn and our family.
Leah, Nathan, Libby, Brian, Kiran, Trevor, Aviana, and Aiden.
I love you all.

Love endures through hardships.

*It [love] always protects, always trusts, always hopes,
always perseveres.*
1 Corinthians 13:7

One

Early January
Nashville, Tennessee

A text from my daughter, Jenny Monroe, read: Turn on Channel 17. Now!

I glanced at Blake Conner in his cute chef's apron while he fried bacon. We'd made plans after our New Year's engagement party the day before to have breakfast together. He stopped by my condo at 6:15 a.m. and brought me to his house. Because this was Wednesday, we planned to go to the office after breakfast.

"Jenny texted me to watch the news. Sounds important." I slipped out of my shoes and rushed to turn on the television in the great room.

I gasped and covered my mouth with my hand. *Eliza's dead? Radnor Lake?* I paused the remote, and it slipped from my hand.

The day before, toward the end of our party, Eliza arrived uninvited and insisted she see me. We spoke for a few minutes. She left angry. Hateful.

I sat on the sofa. *How could she be dead?* I jumped up. *Oh my! I may have been the last person to see her alive.* I twisted to hurry back to the kitchen and saw

Blake rushing toward me.

He touched my arm, his voice edged with concern. "Keedryn, are you okay? What happened? What did Jenny want you to watch?"

Unable to speak, I picked up the remote, rewound the news story, and hit play. The news anchor repeated, "The body of the woman pulled from Radnor Lake last night has been identified as Eliza Walker, age forty-five. A resident of Franklin, she appeared to have drowned. Police are investigating."

Blake took a seat next to me on the couch. He removed the remote from my hand and pulled me close. "Drowned? Her daughter must be devastated."

I rested my head on his shoulder. "Poor Cindy."

"Police are probably investigating whether this was an accident or murder."

"Murder?" I raised my head and brought my hand to my neck. "Why did you say that? She's not one of my favorite people, but why would someone kill her?"

"Don't you suppose she may have gained a few enemies along the way? Look what she did to my family."

Blake referred to recent information exposed that implied Eliza had lied to his deceased wife, Cheryl, which caused her to fall into deep depression.

I jumped up, spun to face him, and groaned. "What if the police think I killed her?"

He cocked his head. "Why would they think that?"

"She came here last night . . . near the end of our party . . . after 4:30. She demanded to talk with me. To tell me I made a horrible mistake."

"Eliza was here? Why didn't you tell me?" He rose and placed his hands on my shoulders.

"I couldn't find you. After she left, I didn't want to ruin our evening by discussing her." I pulled away and paced. When I stopped, I gazed at Blake. "I'm concerned about Allison. She became irate when she saw Eliza leave. I've never seen Allison so upset. What if—?"

"Allison? You're accusing my Allison? Of revenge? My daughter wouldn't do that." His face turned red. I had witnessed his anger less than two weeks earlier. Again, aimed at me. *I hope he'll listen to reason this time and give me a chance to explain.*

"Blake." I drew my eyebrows together. "Not what I meant."

He glared at me and bolted to the kitchen.

I followed and spoke to his back. "Listen to me. I have nothing but love in my heart for your family."

He grabbed his jacket from a hook near the door that led to the garage and spoke in a spiteful tone. "How could you accuse her?" He shook his head and stepped out the door.

I rushed toward him. "Let me explain."

He wheeled around. Faced me. His forehead creased. Eyes narrowed. "You don't need to explain anything. I understand what you meant. We didn't think this engagement through. At least I didn't. You just saved me from a huge mistake." He turned, mumbled something I couldn't make out, and slammed the door in my face.

~

My legs felt like lead. *Did he say, "We didn't think this engagement through?"* I forced myself to open the door and hurried into the garage. Too late. The front of a black Ford 150 backed out from its parking space and down the driveway. The garage door lowered.

I raised my hands in the air and grimaced.

What did he expect me to do? Leave my ring on the kitchen counter? Drive to the office? Finish my two-week notice? Evaporate from his life? I didn't have a car. *Now I'm stuck here. Waiting on Blake to return home. A man who doesn't want me.*

I reached into my pants pocket for my phone to call Jenny to rescue me, but it wasn't there. *Must have left it inside.*

I whirled back to the door to return to the warm house. Locked. The door had a keyless entry pad, but I didn't know the code. I rubbed my arms. I wore a long sleeve blouse but wished I hadn't slipped off my shoes earlier. My socks offered little warmth.

Instead of my focus being on Blake and our relationship, I needed to consider my well-being. How long would I need to stay in the garage? I craved warmth. I scanned the largest and neatest garage I'd ever seen. Upper and lower light blue cabinets lined the wall behind me with a counter in between. Three bicycles were mounted on the far wall. I assumed at least two had not been ridden in the past several years. A large SUV sat in front of me in the garage's third parking spot.

Maybe one of the cabinets holds a house key? I peeked into each one but found nothing. I rested my hand on top of my head and looked at Blake's SUV.

If not a house key, maybe a spare car key in the glove box. I didn't expect to find anything, but I determined to try. Closest to the kitchen door had been the black pickup. The next parking space must have held Blake's BMW, the car he picked me up in that morning and parked in the circular driveway out front.

The next car was the SUV. When I moved closer, I

saw it was an Infiniti. I jumped inside and began my search. The glove box contained the owner's manual and window sticker. Hermosa Blue and brand new. I shook my head. A lot of money to spend on a car. I finished my search and climbed out.

I sighed when I spotted another vehicle hidden behind the SUV. A bright red Ferrari convertible. I didn't bother to look inside because I'd be afraid to drive such a fancy sports car if the keys were in the ignition.

I scurried back to the Infiniti in time to see movement outside the windows that faced the front yard. Light blue sheer curtains hung on these windows. After a well-dressed man and woman peered inside Blake's BMW, the male approached a garage window. Detectives? I jumped into the back passenger seat and ducked out of sight.

The last time the police stopped at my house, I was ten. They told my aunt that my parents had died in an accident.

Should I greet them or stay hidden? The detectives could free me. Give me warmth. Call Jenny. But what if they questioned me? Or took me to jail? No. I'm not ready for questions.

I lay across the seat, pulled my legs into a fetal position, and tried to stop shivering. How long would I be stuck there until Blake came home? Hopefully, he'd be home for lunch. *Almost five hours from now?* My stomach growled. *Oh, no. The bacon. Did he turn off the burner?* I hadn't eaten much at the party the night before and no breakfast that morning. I craved a hot cafe mocha. Did any of that matter though?

What about my relationship with Blake? *Are we really done?*

We'd come so far over the past few months. From a tumultuous relationship at work to one of love and commitment. *And now it's over? Because of one comment I made?* I covered my face with my hands.

How do I make him understand? My concern was for Allison. If anyone witnessed her anger because of Eliza's visit, they could notify the police and implicate her. What if Blake chooses not to believe the truth that I was concerned for her and not accusing her? I sighed and wiped my eyes on my sleeve.

Me, the mistake. I yawned. But we didn't make a mistake. God brought us together, and He'd bring us through. *Right, Lord?*

~

I awoke to a rumbling sound. *Thunder? Is it supposed to rain today? Oh, the garage door.* I peeked at my watch, *9:10*, and then toward Blake's pickup as he pulled into the garage. I expected the Infiniti's tinted windows would keep me hidden from his view. He climbed out, moseyed to the front of the SUV, and laid his hand on the hood. He then strode over to the Ferrari. *Is he checking to find out if I took one of his precious vehicles for a drive?*

When he passed in front of the Infiniti on his way toward the door to the house, I swung open the door.

He jerked his head back and stiffened. "Why are you in the garage?"

I supposed I was a sight since I'd fallen asleep. With my head lifted high, I strutted closer to him. "I followed you out this morning to talk sense into you." I glanced toward the door that led into the kitchen. "And I got locked out."

I needed to check my emotions. Besides being cold

and hungry, concern etched Blake's face when he checked on his SUV and Ferrari. Concern I didn't see on his face for me. His smirk resembled amusement.

"Did you try the code?" His eyes twinkled. "The same one I use for my phone, and you have that." He strolled toward the keyless entry pad and punched in 533379. "Why didn't you call me?"

He opened the door and motioned for me to go first.

"My phone is in the house." *I wouldn't have called you anyway.* I scanned the kitchen to see if I'd left my cell on the counter or table. When I didn't see it there, I took a few steps toward the hallway. "Must be in the great room."

"Go get your phone and listen to your messages. We can talk after." He patted my shoulder.

I strolled down the hallway, past the stairway which led to the second floor, and through the great room. What was going on? I thought he'd want me gone by now. Were we finished, or did he come to his senses? I slipped down the hall and into the bathroom. After I freshened up, I returned to the great room, found my phone on the sofa, shoved it into my pocket, and padded back to the kitchen.

Blake wore his apron again. "I'm preparing another breakfast." He smiled. "Fresh bacon."

I ambled over to the stove and stood next to him. "Take me home. I'll drive to the office and clean out my desk." I removed the ring from my finger and held it in my palm.

He spun me to face him. "What are you doing?"

I turned my head away and bit my lip. I didn't want to cry. His voice held compassion, which confused me. "You said, I'm a mistake." I moved away, plodded toward the backdoor and clutched the ring. "If you don't want to take me home, I'll call Jenny and ask her to pick me up."

Blake pulled me close. "Did you listen to my voicemails?"

I shook my head.

He led me to the kitchen table. "Sit with me, please?"

I plopped into a chair.

He sat next to me. "Jenny and I both tried to reach you this morning. We spoke once and were concerned about you." He nodded and pointed to my phone.

My cell showed six missed calls, six voicemails, and five texts from Jenny. I listened to the voicemails first.

Blake called at 6:52 a.m., a few minutes after he'd left, apologized for his outburst, and asked me to call him as soon as possible. He called at 7:23 and told me again how sorry he was. He needed to attend a meeting at 8:00 and would try me afterward, and he told me where he kept the car keys so I could drive to the office.

Silly me. I should know better than to think he valued his cars more than me. And it didn't take him long at all to realize his mistake and try to fix things.

The next message came from Jenny at 7:51 to ask if I planned to go to the office. She called again at 8:36 and asked, "Where are you?"

Blake called again at 8:45 and said he'd be right home. He sounded concerned.

I pulled at my collar and squirmed. How foolish of me.

Jenny's last call, at 9:05, said she'd check on me later in the afternoon. I peeked at my watch. The time was 9:27. Her texts were much the same. I replied by text: I'm fine. Blake is with me. Explain later.

Blake put his arm around my shoulder.

I jerked away, jumped up, and faced him. "I can't do this. Won't work."

His eyes narrowed. "What? Me? Us? K, I apologized."

I spoke in a frustrated tone. "You got upset with me and didn't give me a chance to explain. Sounded like you wanted me out of your life." I tried to keep my voice calm, but anger exploded. "I can't live in fear that you'll blow up at me whenever I talk to you. How can I share anything with you if I'm afraid you'll get mad at me?" I turned away from him. "This reminds me of when I lived with my Aunt Mary. And I will *never* put myself in that situation again."

His chair squeaked across the floor, and I glanced behind me. He stood and stepped over to a window which faced the backyard and stared out for a silent minute. When he made his way back toward me, he said, "I can't imagine my life without you. I realized that when I drove away this morning." He lifted my chin. "Never doubt my love for you."

I sniffled.

He took my hands in his and brought them to his lips. "There are two things I want you to tell me. I need to understand what your life was like with your Aunt Mary. I want to know everything. And I must know what happened yesterday when Eliza was here." Blake kissed the top of my head. "But first, let's start this day over. Will you sit with me at the table and pray with me?"

His request humbled me. He prayed for our relationship and families. Something he wouldn't have done with me until a week ago. And I looked forward to praying with him for years to come.

I slipped the ring back on my finger. Blake gave me his full attention while I explained my comment from earlier about Allison. Distraught over the news of Eliza's death, and not in the mood to discuss my aunt, I asked if we could put those topics off until later that day.

Blake stood. "I have something for you." He walked to the counter and picked up a coffee mug. He carried it over to the table and deposited the cup into my hands. "Let me heat this for you. I made it before I fixed the second round of bacon."

I stared at the drink. "A cafe mocha?" I looked at Blake.

He smiled.

"You made *me* coffee?" On most days as his assistant, I fetched his coffee. Today, he made mine.

I rose, tilted my head, and gazed into his big blue eyes. I brought the cup to my lips and took a sip. "Good will soon become excellent after you warm this." But I no longer needed coffee. I grinned and moved closer to steal a kiss. A warm, delicious kiss.

Two

Blake continued to prepare breakfast, and at 9:45 he suggested that I tour the second floor of his house on my own. I'd already seen his recording studio. But I'd only peeked into the bedrooms and bathrooms when I went down the hallway the night of our executive's Christmas party two and a half weeks earlier. I made my way to the master suite.

A room fit for a queen. Dark hardwood floors and a stone fireplace complemented the decor. Besides the bed and a cream-colored love seat, a sitting area with two matching chairs and a small round table, sat off to the side of the room. This area included a set of French doors which led to a covered deck with a view of the backyard. I stole a glance outside and noticed a greenhouse, gazebo, bushes, many bare trees, and a pool. Springtime must be lovely. The master bath was next, and it outdid any bathroom I'd ever seen.

No bed and bath magazine came close. Not only marble vanities but marble floors, a sunken tub in the center of the room, and a decorative beige-toned tiled shower. The light green walls with white cabinets and live plants placed around the room reminded me of a tropical paradise. I'd enjoy the makeup area and plush chair when this became mine.

My cell pinged a text from Blake: **Breakfast is ready**. I took the back stairs down to the kitchen.

"Have a seat. Scrambled eggs with cheese coming right up." He brought over a plate of bacon and a pitcher of orange juice and set them on the table.

Yes, a queen. "This isn't your best idea. After we're married, I'll expect this treatment every day."

"My chef will be happy to serve you." He grinned. "Did you find everything satisfactory upstairs?"

I nodded. "Nicki will love the master bath. When she spends the night, she fills the tub like it's her personal spa."

"I hope your granddaughter will spend a lot of time with us." He sat next to me with the bowl of eggs and a plate of buttered toast. "She needs to come over and check out the hot tub and sauna downstairs."

"Downstairs? Hot tub and sauna?" This was news to me. "What else is down there?"

"Let's offer thanks. Would you like to pray?"

After a quick prayer, I eyed Blake and shook my head. "Looks like I need a tour of your entire mansion soon. Roxie will appreciate all the new places to hide."

"Roxie? Cats don't need the run of the entire house. She'll love the basement. Her new home." He took a bite of food and complimented himself on his cooking.

"You plan to confine my Roxie to the basement?" I pursed my lips and gave him my best pouty face.

He chuckled. "Not like it's a dungeon down there. Now eat your eggs before they get cold. You're wasting away worrying about your cat."

After our brunch, I offered to tidy the kitchen and

load the dishwasher.

A few minutes later, Blake retrieved my jacket and escorted me to the garage. He asked me to open my hands, and when I obliged, he placed a set of car keys in my palms. Keys for the Infiniti.

"I'd rather you drive. That's a lot of car for me." I tried to return the keys.

He flinched. "But . . . it's a gift. I bought this for you." He moved to the front of the SUV and glanced at the Ferrari. "Would you rather have . . ."

"No." I lifted my palm. "I appreciate that you thought to buy me a new car, but I'm happy with my Malibu. I don't need anything else. Except maybe a parking space in the garage when we're married." I winked. "Now that would be fine."

"K, you shouldn't turn down a gift. If you don't want the Infiniti, I'll purchase something else. But I want to buy you a new car as my engagement gift to you." His shoulders drooped and he shook his head. He led me back through the house to the front yard and we climbed into his BMW. "I'll take you home to get your Malibu, and we'll go out this weekend to find whatever you want. Think it over."

"I've thought about it. I don't want or need a new car."

"That's not what I meant. When I said 'Think it over' I meant consider what kind of car you want. Not *if* you want. I'm buying you a car."

Why is he being stubborn? I raised my voice. "What you're saying is, I don't have a say in this."

He huffed. "Why do you always have to be stubborn?"

"Me always stubborn?" I crossed my arms and

stared out the windshield. *Another fight? This is ridiculous.* If he wanted to buy me a car, I should let him buy me a car.

He stopped the BMW before we got to the road, reached over, and touched my arm. "Keep your Malibu. Let me know when you want a new vehicle."

"One like Allison's and Jim's. With heated seats." I turned to look at Blake with my eyes opened wide but held my breath and awaited his response.

"Now or later?"

I squeaked out a now.

He snickered. "You can have any car you want, and you're asking me for a Ford Escape?"

"Is there anything wrong with that?"

"Nope. I will buy you a top-of-the-line Escape. Anything else?"

"A red one?"

He sighed. "I'll keep the Infiniti and sell this." He patted the dash. "We'll need the extra room in the Infiniti to take Tim, Nicki, and our new grandbaby places when Andy and Zoey move back."

Tim was Blake's grandson, Allison and Jim's only child. Andy lived in New Mexico, with his girlfriend, Zoey. They were expecting their first child and planned to move to Nashville soon and have a double wedding ceremony with us.

"Did Andy and Zoey get off okay this morning?"

"Allison took them to the airport. Andy told me he'd text me when they got back to Albuquerque."

Fifteen minutes later, we pulled into my condo's parking area and parked next to a dark sedan. Two detectives—one male, one female—greeted us when we climbed out.

~

"Keedryn Reynolds?" The forty-something male detective waited for my response.

I tried to speak but couldn't form my words.

Blake dashed to my side, held my elbow, and whispered. "You're pale."

I nodded at the detective.

The female ambled closer and showed me her identification. "I'm Detective Fields and this is Detective Jacoby. May we have a few minutes of your time?" She fixed her eyes on Blake. "I presume you're Blake Conner?"

"That's correct." Blake led the way to my front door while I rummaged through my purse to find my keys. *This would be a lot easier if my hands weren't shaking.*

I unlocked the door and invited our guests inside. Roxie, perched atop the kitchen counter, jumped off and fled down the hall. I winced. Blake would insist she stay in the basement after seeing her on my counter— something she seldom did. But I had bigger things to worry about.

If I were the last person to see Eliza alive, I could probably be a main suspect. I took a deep breath. *The Lord is with me. Just stay calm.* "May I offer you something to drink?"

Everyone said no, but I excused myself. I needed a sip of water. With the open layout of my condo, I could listen in on their conversation. My living room was small and held a sofa, where the detectives sat, a recliner, and my big, comfy rocker. Blake took a seat in the recliner and left the rocking chair for me. I joined them a minute later.

Blake told the detectives he heard the report on the

news that morning and asked about Eliza's daughter, Cindy, and if there was any new information.

Fields said, "Nothing I can disclose." She looked at me. "And when did you receive the news?"

"A few minutes before Blake."

She narrowed her eyes and observed her partner before she returned her gaze to us. "We understand the two of you held an engagement party yesterday. And a few days before that Ms. Walker was engaged . . ." She peered at Blake. "To you, sir. When was the last time you saw Eliza Walker?"

"Last Friday. Around 9:30 a.m."

"What took place that morning?"

"I broke off our engagement." Blake held his head high, his demeanor confident.

She focused on me. "When was the last time you saw Ms. Walker?"

I glanced toward the thermostat and tugged my collar. "She arrived at Blake's house around 4:30 p.m. yesterday. Our party was winding down. She wanted to talk with me."

"Who else saw her while she was in Mr. Conner's home?"

"My daughter Jenny Monroe and her husband Carl. He let Eliza inside and stayed with her in the front sitting room until Jenny found me in the great room where we held the party." I made eye contact with each detective and kept my tone light and conversational. "Blake's daughter Allison saw Eliza leave. Other than the four of us, I don't know if anyone else noticed she was there." I didn't want to raise questions regarding Allison's reaction.

Jacoby asked, "What did you and Ms. Walker talk

about?"

I hesitated because I hadn't shared that conversation with Blake. I stared at him and raised my eyebrows. My stomach churned. I wanted him to tell me what to do. I jumped up. "Excuse me. I need a glass of water." I dashed into the kitchen.

Blake said, "Detectives, Keedryn is rather shaken by the news of Ms. Walker's death, and your presence here is causing her additional anxiety regarding her past." He then told them about how I was told of my parent's death by two officers who came to my door when I was young. Blake stood. "Excuse me while I check on her." He cleared his throat. "On second thought, unless one of us is a suspect in the death of Ms. Walker, we are finished answering your questions."

I brought my hand up to my neck. *Can he do that? Won't they assume that we have something to hide?*

Blake entered the kitchen. "Are you okay?"

"Yes, but I need to tell you what happened first."

"I'll send them off. We gave them consent to ask questions by inviting them inside, but we've told them everything they must know. They don't need your private conversation."

Blake walked toward the living room. "If you have further questions, please contact my attorney." He took out his cell and gave them his lawyer's name and number.

I stepped into the living room when the detectives rose.

Jacoby said, "We do have more questions, and we'll need a copy of your guest list." The detectives strode to the door, and after Blake saw them out, I collapsed on the sofa.

~

Blake held me close. "You did great. I know the question about who else saw Eliza yesterday was tough, but you handled it with grace and ease." He kissed me and ran his finger along my cheek. "Now tell me what happened. What was Eliza's motive to crash our engagement party?" He held my hand and squeezed.

I whispered a prayer. I didn't want to get Blake upset again, and I didn't want him to think he would soon marry a loony woman. "She accused you of infidelity while married to Cheryl. Nothing new with her accusation except I threw the lie back in her face. She didn't expect that."

"What did you say to her?"

"Eliza wanted to blame you for everything that happened." I looked straight ahead. I'd done my best to block out that conversation. Her screaming. Ranting. The evil look in her eyes.

Blake shook my shoulder. "K?"

I stood. "She . . . she." I stared at the floor. "I don't know how to describe what took place without sounding kooky. Even if you believe me, the police might lock me up." I turned toward Blake.

He rose and wrapped his arms around me. "Start at the beginning. Tell me everything." He led me back to the sofa.

"Carl waited outside the sitting room and watched through the French doors to stand guard in case things got ugly. I prayed, pulled back my shoulders, and said, 'What can I do for you this evening, Eliza?'

"Evil eyes glared at me. She spouted off. 'You know you plan to marry a man who will be unfaithful to you. He'll never change. Unfaithful to Cheryl. Unfaithful to you.'"

My body trembled. Blake pulled me as close as he could. His embrace helped me continue.

"I said, 'Eliza, do you realize the part you played in Cheryl's depression? Her mental condition came from the lies you fed her over several months. Her journals prove it.'

"She shoved me away and denied that she told Cheryl lies.

"'I want you to know,' I told her, 'I forgive you.' Fury radiated from her dark eyes.

"She got close to my face and said, 'Why would *you* need to forgive *me*?'

"I said, 'I forgive you for coming here today to disrupt my engagement party. I forgive you for trying to steal Blake away from me and for the lies you told Cheryl, Blake, and their family.'"

Blake kissed the top of my head and caressed my hair.

"'But it's not my forgiveness you need. You need the Lord's forgiveness.'

"She spewed profanities, jerked around the room with her arms thrashing about, and screamed at the top of her lungs. 'No. No. No.' Carl opened the door and Eliza ran past him and out the front door looking up with her hands covering her head."

Blake turned my chin toward him. "Did she hurt you?"

"No. Only the shove. All I remember. Carl appeared stunned when he came into the sitting room, though. He said he tried to enter sooner but couldn't get the door opened. He asked me several times if I was okay."

"What do you suppose happened to Eliza?"

"Who knows?" My voice shook. "She acted crazy. And now she's dead."

Three

Blake left for the office at noon to finish a few things and suggested I take the day off and rest. He said he wouldn't be long.

Instead, I tidied my home. Housework helped to get my mind off Eliza.

As promised, Jenny called around 3:00. "I was concerned for you last night after Carl told me what happened. He was afraid Eliza broke your ribs when she shoved you."

"She didn't shove me *that* hard."

Jenny sighed. "I just parked out front because I want to see for myself that you're okay."

I met her on my front porch, we hugged, and entered my condo. "Have the police questioned you yet?"

"When I stopped at the house after my morning errands, my neighbor told me a dark car pulled into my driveway earlier and a well-dressed man and woman knocked on my front door. I presume they'll be back." Jenny dropped her purse on the sofa and took a seat.

My front door opened, and Blake came inside with a small wrapped gift.

After Jenny greeted him, she peered at me. "And what happened to you this morning? Why didn't you him. "Talk to me."

"I'm being silly. I feel like something's not right."

"Because I got upset yesterday?" He took both of my hands in his. "I did better. Two weeks ago, when I got angry, I didn't apologize until five days later. Yesterday, I realized my mistake and called you within five minutes."

"You did much better." I smiled. "But that's not it."

"I know what you need." He dipped his head and kissed my cheek. "I love you. Don't you forget it."

"I feel better already, so time for me to get to work." I slipped out of his office and rushed to my desk. When I turned on my computer, I saw the job posting on our Intranet, dated the Friday before, for my current position—the one I'd resigned. I let out a lengthy sigh. Today was the last day for internal applicants to notify HR of their interest. All interviews would take place the next day. Would any of the applicants be able to deal with Blake's moods?

~

Blake and I enjoyed a pleasant lunch together at a nearby barbeque place. We chatted about his conversation with his attorney who assured Blake the investigation was standard and most likely Eliza's death was accidental. Blake also suggested that we make wedding plans.

"I guess the first thing to do is to set a definite date." I bounced the heels of my shoes up and down on the floor.

"We talked about getting married before Andy and Zoey's baby was due—mid-March, right?"

I nodded and pulled up my phone calendar. "The latest we could marry, in case the baby arrives a week respond to my calls and texts?"

"Let me answer that." Blake placed the gift on the coffee table.

"I can answer for myself." I sat in my rocker. "But before I do, does being engaged mean I can walk into your house whenever I want?"

"Sure does. You have the code—no reason to knock." He smiled.

"I prefer to alert you of my arrival and for you to use my doorbell." I smirked.

"Ouch." He saluted me and bent down to kiss my cheek.

My attention returned to Jenny, and I told her about my time spent locked in Blake's garage. "I was freezing and starving."

Blake chuckled. "Freezing in a heated garage?"

"What heat?"

"I keep the garage at fifty-five degrees in the winter. Keeps my vehicles happy and healthy."

"Well, it felt a lot colder." I narrowed my eyes. "Trying to make me look bad in front of my daughter?"

He glanced at Jenny. "She has the code to the keyless entry but didn't think to use it." His eyes crinkled at the corners.

"That's enough, Mr. Conner."

He pulled me out of my chair and wrapped me in his arms. "May I kiss you in front of your daughter?"

Jenny giggled. "Won't bother me in the least."

After our kiss, I stared at the gift he brought. "A peace offering?"

"I concluded that might be an excellent idea." He picked up the slender package and handed it to me.

I suspected jewelry of some sort and pulled off the

ribbon to unwrap the gift.

Jenny stood and came closer. "I want to see."

When I removed the lid, I found a white gold, diamond heart pendant necklace. "Oh, Blake." I placed my hand on my neck, sure this was the real deal. "If you buy me expensive gifts after every spat, you'll be bankrupt before we hit our tenth anniversary."

I don't know who laughed louder—Jenny or Blake.

Jenny pulled her phone out of her pocket and frowned. "Carl texted me and said to call him now. I hope he and Nicki are okay."

After her call to Carl, Jenny bolted out the door. Something about Nicki broke her silence.

Blake followed Jenny to the door and pushed it closed after he told her goodbye. "What do you suppose she meant by that?"

"She was probably referring to a secret Nicki could no longer keep." I patted my tummy.

"Goodness no. She told Carl her Nana's pregnant?"

"Not me, you goofy man." I shook my head and slapped him on his arm.

~

Blake removed the necklace from the box and stared at it. "K, I'm so sorry about this morning. The more I think about it, the more irritated with myself I become." He gazed into my eyes. "I know you love Allison and Andy too." He slid behind me, brushed the hair from my neck and clasped the hook. "Do you like it?" He leaned down and kissed my cheek.

I turned with tears in my eyes. "Beautiful."

"Are you okay? I didn't mean to upset you."

I cupped his cheek in my palm. "You're forgiven for this morning." I looked down at my necklace and fingered the heart pendant. "The last memory I have of my parents." I fought my emotions. "My dad put a string of pearls around Mama's neck, and he kissed her cheek before they left for their anniversary dinner." I reached into my pocket and pulled out a tissue.

Blake held me close. "Had I realized, I would have given you something else."

I pulled back to see his face. "This is perfect. I love it. But I was happy with the roses too."

He pushed my hair behind my ear. "I believe you were. But I thought you might prefer something different—something unique for Keedryn."

I sighed and stepped back. "Does this mean I'll never get another rose?"

"If you want roses, you'll get roses. I have a new variety in my greenhouse, which should be available soon." His eyes twinkled. "They'll be perfect for you."

"I can't wait to see them." I led him by the hand to my sofa. "You know a little about my family, but I don't know much about yours. Are your parents' living?"

"Only Mom. My dad died twenty years ago." He squeezed my hand. "And I have a sister, Lydia, who lives in Europe. I haven't seen her for a few years."

"Where does your mom live?"

"Florida. When Aunt Debra retired as my assistant last summer, she moved in with Mom."

"Florida? I don't remember you traveling there recently. Did you see them over the holidays?"

He shook his head. "They took a cruise."

A worship song played on his phone. He answered the call. "Hi, Allison. . . I'm with Keedryn at her condo. . . Yes, we heard the news. . . Calm down. . . Come over at 5:30 . . . We'll order pizza. We can talk this through. .

. See you soon." He disconnected the call. "She's a mess. I hope you don't mind that I invited her and her family over for dinner."

"Not at all. None of us expected anything like this to happen to Eliza. Might be good if Jenny and Carl join us too. I'll call them." My chest tightened. *Carl witnessed my encounter with Eliza. Maybe he can shed some light on her visit.*

~

Allison, her husband Jim, and their son Tim arrived a few minutes after Jenny, Carl, and my granddaughter Nicki. Seating was tight in my small condo. My table seated four. Nicki didn't want to leave Papa Blake, but we convinced her that Tim didn't want to eat alone in the TV room. Jim and Carl sat on the floor along the wall next to the table in my dining area.

"This is horrible. I wasn't fond of Eliza. But I never wished her dead," Allison stared out the window to the backyard. "Anyone know what happened?"

Blake stood and ambled to the counter for another slice of pizza. "I don't think the police know anything yet. Have they questioned you?"

"No. Why would they?" She squirmed, gawked at Blake, and scrunched her face.

I reached across the table toward her hand. "I told them the only people who saw Eliza last night, as far as I knew, were Jenny, Carl, and you."

Allison peered at Jenny. "Have they questioned you?"

"I wasn't home. But Carl talked to them."

All eyes darted to Carl. He rose and shook out his legs. "I was brief with them. Eliza arrived. Jenny found Keedryn. And they talked. I told them her arrival time.

And when she left. That's all." He rubbed the back of his neck.

Jenny giggled. "Tell them what happened the way you told me." She glanced around at each one of us. "He used his children's pastor story-telling technique."

Carl widened his eyes and spoke in an animated tone as he would if he was teaching a lesson at church. "Eliza arrived when the party was wrapping up. She insisted she speak to Keedryn, but I offered to find Blake. She wanted nothing to do with him." He gazed at me. "When Jenny brought you to the sitting room, I remained outside the French doors and kept watch. Eliza shoved you and you stumbled."

I tilted my head. "I don't remember stumbling."

"Didn't seem to faze you in the least. You got right in her face. But you kept your cool." Carl ran his hand through his hair. "Eliza didn't seem to respond well to whatever you told her. She appeared agitated and flung her arms around." Carl mimicked her motions. "I tried to open the door, but it seemed to be locked. I was afraid she might hurt you." He stared at the floor. "I felt helpless." He wiped his brow with the back of his hand.

I shook my head. "But you got the door open, and Eliza ran outside." I stood and touched Carl on the shoulder.

He used his normal voice and relaxed his stance. "Yeah. After several tries, it came open. She took off like a scared chicken."

"Did you go straight home after you left Blake's?" I glanced back and forth between Carl and Jenny.

They both nodded.

Blake looked at Allison. "You'll need to answer the detectives' questions as soon as tomorrow. What time did you leave after the party and where did you go?"

"We went straight home, too, along with Andy and Zoey—left your place after we helped with cleanup. Which means we have witnesses until 6:00—Tauni and Wes—because they stayed to help tear down tables and move furniture."

Blake rubbed his chin. "Walt's another witness. He took a call in the sitting room and said goodbye around 6:00."

Tauni Fisher and Wes Thomas worked with us at Boden Combs Healthcare, and I considered them both friends. Walt Watson was the chairman of the board and a friend of Blake's.

Jim rose and moved in behind Allison and massaged her shoulders. "We played Scrabble upstairs in the bonus room and turned in for the night. Andy and Zoey needed to catch an early flight this morning."

"Great," Blake said. "So, the four of you played a game and remained home all night."

"Not the four of us. Zoey played, but Andy stayed downstairs and watched a movie on Netflix."

Could Andy have slipped out with no one knowing? I wasn't about to ask that question out loud.

After we cleaned up the kitchen and said our goodbyes, Nicki whispered in Jenny's ear. She smiled and patted Nicki's head. "Yes, you may tell them our news."

Nicki jumped up and down and clapped. "We're having a baby. Just a boy, but I guess that will be okay."

We all laughed and congratulated my daughter, Carl, and Nicki.

Jim took Allison by the hand. "Come on, beautiful. Let's go home to our warm little castle." He ruffled

Tim's hair. "You ready, buddy?"

Blake closed the door behind them and gathered me in his arms. "I owe you an apology."

I spoke in a scolding tone. "What now?"

"Your story earlier about Eliza sounded a little crazy. But Carl's description agrees with yours. That woman was . . ." Blake rubbed his hand down his face, "evil."

Four

The following day, a Thursday, and while I drove to the office, I questioned whether I should stay at BCH or search for another job. I resigned the week before after Blake became engaged to Eliza. Although that was no longer the situation, the company had enforced a new policy that stated an employee and their supervisor could not date. A new position was available that Chad Warren, our company president, asked me to consider—an HR generalist.

After I placed my purse in my desk's bottom drawer, I took off down the hall to visit Jocelyn Lancaster, our new HR director.

She rose and stuck out her hand. "I'm happy to see you. I've had no other internal applicants, so the job is yours if you want it." She brought her palms together under her chin. "Please say yes."

"I believe I understand what the position involves, but I'd like a brief rundown. I worked part-time in a human resource capacity many years ago but know things have changed."

"You'll oversee the interviewing and hiring of new employees and their onboarding process after they're hired." Jocelyn took in a deep breath, sat, and tapped her pen up and down on her desk. "You'll also manage employee training records, update company policies and procedures, and handle benefits, leave time, and employee complaints. And you'll work with the Accounting Department to make sure they get all the information they need to process payroll." She shuffled a few forms on her desk.

"I'm interested—"

"Oh, that's great." She jumped up.

"I didn't say yes, yet. Will it be okay if I let you know tomorrow?" I gnawed on my lower lip. "I'd like to discuss this with Blake one more time."

She took her seat again, scribbled something on a piece of paper, folded it over, and handed it to me. "Chad's my supervisor and I'll be yours. There's no problem with the dating policy. You're free to date and marry, Blake." She grinned and nodded toward the paper. "What do you think of the offer?"

I opened the folded paper and gasped. "This is more than my last increase. I'll let you know tomorrow morning when I arrive."

Jocelyn stepped to the front of her desk. "I'll look forward to your yes, and I'll have an official offer letter ready for you tomorrow."

I left her office and dashed into the employee breakroom to grab Blake a cup of coffee and cream. Beth Davis, Chad's executive assistant and my best friend at work, stood at the counter making herself a cup of tea. I welcomed her back from her time off, thanked her for attending our engagement party, and updated her on my job situation. "I'm concerned about taking the HR position. Maybe I should make a clean break and find a job elsewhere. What do you think?"

She raised her eyebrows and threw her tea bag in the trash. "You should stay here. I'll miss you if you leave."

"Sweet, but I'm not sure that's best. What if I don't enjoy the HR position? So much to relearn."

"You'll do fine. But if you're unsure, spend extra time on your knees."

"You're right." I thanked her and darted to our office suite with a coffee cup in hand.

Although I'd only been Blake's assistant for seven months, a whirlwind of emotions overtook me. I glanced around my office area and strolled into his. I'd either leave BCH for good or move down the hall. Either way, I'd grown attached to sharing this office suite with Blake. *Silly. You'll soon share his home.* I placed the coffee cup on his desk and presumed he'd arrive soon.

"Keedryn."

I spun on my heels and there stood Blake. "I. . . I brought you a cup of coffee."

He tilted back his head and laughed. "You look like you did the first time you brought me coffee and spilled it all over my shoes. What's up?"

"Not sure. I'm being nostalgic this morning. I spoke to Jocelyn and told her that I'd get with her tomorrow regarding whether I'll take the HR position. But when I came back into our office suite, I felt overwhelmed." I shook my head. "Things are changing fast."

"And you wanted to get married two days ago. How would you feel right now if we'd carried out those plans?"

I stared at him.

"Come have a seat at the table." He led me by my elbow to his round, mahogany conference table and I sat. He took a seat next to me and turned my chin toward

early, will be the first weekend in March. But that's close to Cheryl's. . ."

He reached across the table and touched my hand. "Thank you for being sensitive to her passing. That date might freak Andy out a little too much."

"Agreed." I leaned back in my chair, and Blake released my hand.

"Rather soon, but what about Valentine's weekend?" he said.

"Too commercialized. We could get married the week after."

"Seven weeks. Is that enough time for you to plan a wedding?"

I held my breath for a moment and spoke with frustration. "Not really. To pull that off, Andy and Zoey need to move here soon. How can we have a double wedding without them?"

He peered at his phone—his brows furrowed.

I straightened. "What is it?"

"A text from our receptionist. The police are at the office with a warrant to search my BMW."

~

Blake parked his BMW in BCH's lot and jumped out. He bolted for the door, and I jogged after him. Inside, he approached Detectives Jacoby and Fields and spoke in an irritated tone. "What's this about a search warrant and my car?"

Jacoby handed Blake a copy of the warrant.

Blake whirled in the opposite direction and walked outside. The detectives and I followed. "I don't appreciate your coming to my place of work. You should have brought this with you yesterday and taken care of it. Not here at my company and with employees gawking." He trudged to his BMW and unlocked it. "What are you looking for?"

Fields said, "Someone saw a dark car outside Radnor Lake's eastside gated entrance Tuesday evening. The description matches your BMW. We noticed yesterday the mud on your tires and the tire tracks at the scene. We didn't get the warrant until this morning."

"Mud? This is Nashville, Tennessee. We have mud."

I brushed my fingers down Blake's arm, hoping to calm him.

"Mr. Conner, we're just doing our job. Excuse me." She joined Jacoby, who scraped mud from Blake's tires and placed it into an evidence bag. Fields took pictures of the car and tires.

The detectives did a brief search inside the vehicle and wrapped up in twenty minutes. They thanked Blake and left.

Blake wheeled around toward me. "Can you believe that?" He shook his head and paced.

I reached for his hand when he strode past. "Do any other family members have a dark car—similar in style? I hope no one else has to deal with a search."

"Jim has the Escape and Allison drives a silver Camry."

"Carl owns a Honda CR-V, Jenny has a Ford Focus, and I have the white Malibu. Which means we have nothing more to concern us. None of those match the description."

"Only mine. And I didn't go anywhere after the party."

We took a few steps toward the employee entrance and stopped.

"I don't remember any of our family members leaving before or soon after the party ended, do you?" I said.

"They all stayed until we finished cleaning and left around 6:00. There shouldn't be any question about any of us since everyone went straight home."

"Except me. I stayed at your place until 8:00." I glanced back at Blake's car. "Unless. . ."

"Unless what?" Blake glared at me.

"Nothing. Nothing at all." *I don't dare share my thoughts.*

"Let's get to my office and out of the cold. I want to know what you don't want to tell me."

We hurried inside the building, and Blake headed toward the elevator while I made my way to the stairs. "I'll be there soon." I needed a few minutes to think and pray.

~

"Keedryn." I peeked up from my computer and saw Blake on the other side of my desk. "My office."

Inside, I sat at his conference table.

He closed his office door and took a seat next to me. "Unless what?"

At least his demeanor softened since I'd made the comment outside. "Like I said, nothing at all."

He bent his head down and gazed at me from the top of his eyes.

I smiled as sweetly as possible.

"K, I won't get upset. You dangled a thought and I'd like to hear it." He took my hand and squeezed. I stared at the table. "What if, since everyone was upstairs at Allison's, Andy slipped out with no one noticing?"

Blake released my hand and jumped up.

I glanced at him and wrinkled my forehead. "Is that at all possible? In case the police ask?"

He spoke in a stern tone. "Why does your mind go to the worst-case scenario?" He shook his fist. "Do you watch crime shows every evening?"

I brought my hand up to my mouth, shook my head, and stood. "The idea came quick. I spoke too soon. When I realized how wacky the idea was, I didn't want to tell you. You talked all sweet and promised not to get upset. But now you're angry with me. Again." I opened his office door and raised my voice. "I'm going home, and I'll see you tomorrow."

"But it's only 1:45, and I have a letter for you to complete."

"Do it yourself."

Five

I called Beth before I left the parking lot and told her to expect a letter from Blake.

She laughed when I told her what happened. "You couldn't have gotten away with that a few months ago, but I'll bet you wanted to say that and more."

"That's an understatement." I chuckled too. "You should have seen his face. Shocked doesn't do it justice. He gaped at me, wrinkled his forehead, and took a wide stance with his fists on his hips. Quite a sight."

After dinner, Roxie and I snuggled on the sofa in the TV room. I picked up my Bible, read several passages from Psalms, and prayed. *Lord, will Blake and I make it as a couple? I have my doubts. Lead us in Your plan and guide me as to if I should find a job outside of BCH. To see him throughout the day at work and at home may be too much together time. I'm not sure our marriage can endure that.*

The doorbell rang, and I rushed to peek out my front window—Blake. I should have known he'd stop by. I moseyed to the door to let him inside.

"Did you know it's snowing out there?" He brushed off his jacket. "I won't stay long. I need to go to the store for bread and milk." He dipped his head toward my cheek.

I took a step back and motioned him to the couch. "Let me take your coat." I placed it on the back of the recliner and sat in my rocking chair.

"You're still upset with me, aren't you?" he asked. "I should be perturbed with you. You understand I could fire you for walking out today—especially when you told me I could finalize my letter. That's no way to talk to your boss." He tilted his head and grinned.

"In case you've forgotten. . ." I folded my arms across my chest. "I resigned."

"What? You've decided not to take the HR position?"

I glanced toward the front window. "Perhaps it would be better for our marriage if we didn't see each other throughout the day. I don't want everyone to realize when we've had a spat. Might be best if I look elsewhere."

He cocked his head. "Are you sure that's what you want?"

"I don't know what I want." I glared at Blake. "But I need to give Jocelyn my answer tomorrow."

"You worry too much. Everything will be fine." He patted the sofa seat to his right. "Please?"

"I'll stay here." I shook my head. "Why did you stop by?"

He jerked his head back and stiffened. "I love you. Why wouldn't I stop by?"

"Because you were angry with me."

"Oh, that. I would have come sooner to apologize— again—but I got stopped by Detectives Fields and Jacoby. They were waiting for me at my house when I got home. They needed Andy's phone number." He patted the cushion again.

I didn't move.

"Let me tell you this. I considered what you'd said about Andy. He got upset when he was here for Christmas and we first discussed Cheryl's journal entries. He was ready to punch something—anything." Blake sat back and crossed his left ankle over his right knee. "If he saw Eliza in his mother's home again, he may have reacted recklessly. Not murder—I would never expect that—but possibly display anger."

I rocked in my chair.

"I talked to Allison. She and Jim each had their car keys, so Andy had no transportation available except to walk. Besides, they heard him downstairs singing." Blake leaned closer. "I've got to ask, though. Neither of their cars fit the description. What were you thinking?"

"He could have come by your place and gotten your car. He knows the code and where you keep the extra keys. In your enormous house, he might have slipped in and out without you knowing." I stood and plopped on the sofa next to Blake. "What did you learn from the police detectives?"

"They didn't share much. Most of what I found out came from my attorney, Matt Starnes. He has a source at the police station."

"A snitch?" I giggled.

"Something like that. Although an autopsy was requested, the report isn't finished. But they calculated the time of death between 4:00 and 6:00 p.m. Tuesday evening." He shook his head and held my hand. "This is why our family looks suspicious. Cindy knew her mom planned to stop by my place to see you that evening. Which makes it important for the police to know if any of us left the party."

"But we have witnesses, and the entire family was together until 6:00." I wrapped my arms around Blake's waist. "Did the detectives say anything about your car?"

He chuckled. "There was a dark BMW parked at the gate. The police found out this afternoon, after they searched my car, that a man came back after the park closed to find his granddaughter's stuffed elephant. She dropped it in the parking lot and cried when she got home and realized it was gone."

I pulled away and looked at him. "I guess that means we're in the clear now. At least this part of our lives will get back to normal. Now we can plan our double wedding."

"The police may still need to talk with Wes, Tauni, and Walt, but there shouldn't be any issues there." He arched his brow and crossed his arms.

~

Friday morning, I slipped into Jocelyn's office. Time to tell her I didn't plan to stay.

She leapt out of her chair and embraced me. "Please say yes. You're perfect for this job, and I need you." I squirmed and she lowered her hands to her sides. "Apologies for my exuberance, but I'm overwhelmed right now and could use your help."

I smiled and pointed toward the neighboring office. "I planned to tell you no, but you seem desperate. Okay, if I move in today?"

She raised both hands upward. "Yes. Thank you." She grabbed an envelope from her desk. "Here's your offer letter." She told me about three interviews scheduled with admins who'd applied for Blake's executive assistant. We'd meet with Alicia from

Marketing at 10:30, Tauni from Insurance at 1:00, and Terri from Legal at 2:00.

I envisioned a busy day ahead of me and dashed down the hall to my old office to throw personal items into a box.

When Blake came into our offices, he stopped at my desk. "Are you leaving or moving? I thought I'd have you here through next Tuesday."

I rubbed my hands together in my lap. "Moving."

His eyes twinkled. "That's great. Are we on for lunch today?"

"Can we discuss our wedding plans?"

"Sounds perfect." He strode into his office.

I hurried in after him. "Jocelyn and I are interviewing today. Do you want to take part? Or is that too petty for you?"

He twisted his mouth. "Do you need me? Promote whomever you deem the best candidate for the position."

"Will do." Although I was moving things down the hall, I told Blake I'd assist him with whatever he needed during our transitional time.

I finished packing and carried my belongings to my new office—smaller but more private, with a connecting door into Jocelyn's office. The floor to ceiling window, which looked out into the hallway, added security if I were in the room alone with an upset employee. I scanned my walls and planned to add three photos or plaques to make the place mine—if I chose to stay.

~

Jocelyn asked me to take the lead with the interviews. Alicia surprised me with her quick and detailed responses. After difficulties when I worked with her on a project a month earlier, she impressed me with the way she handled herself. Maybe I misjudged her.

Blake and I met at the elevator at 11:45 and left for lunch. He took me to the same Chinese restaurant he'd taken me to for our first business lunch. We both commented on the improvement they'd made over the past few months—new cushioned seats in the booths. I tossed my purse onto the cushion next to me and slid into my seat.

Blake took the seat across from me and grinned. "I'm glad to see you're comfortable with me now." He glanced at my purse next to me. The first time we endured lunch together, I clutched my purse in my lap to protect me from my mean and arrogant boss.

"I better be relaxed if I plan to marry you soon."

He pushed his menu aside. "Let's pick a date, and I'll call Andy and see if it works for him and Zoey."

"We talked about February 23 if we can arrange everything before Zoey delivers. I guess we need to look at April if we need to wait—possibly the thirteenth? The baby will be about four weeks old." I frowned. My desire was for them to get married before the baby was born.

We ordered our food and Blake took out his cell. "I'll step outside for a few minutes where it's quieter and give Andy a call."

I pulled out my phone and read a few emails.

My cell pinged with a text message from Zoey: Andy on call with Blake. Told him not moving. No double wedding. What's happening? She included a crying emoji.

What in the world? Three days before, Andy told Blake that he and Zoey would move to Nashville soon. I texted her back: Misunderstanding? Don't worry. They'll work this out.

The server brought our food, but Blake hadn't returned. I prayed for him and Andy while they discussed this over the phone.

When Blake rejoined me, his eyes looked weary. He slumped into his seat. "I don't understand what just happened." He shook his head. "First he told me that they both lost their jobs at the restaurant when they stayed the extra days."

"Then there's no reason for them not to move now. Andy can look for work here in town."

"You'd think so. But Andy said they're not moving back. I couldn't say anything to convince him this was where he and Zoey should live. He sounded angry with me."

"Because of me. Blake, I'm sorry. This is my fault. Andy resents me—not you."

Am I worth the cost of losing his son?

He gazed at me. "This isn't your fault. And if he has a problem with you, he has a problem with me." He reached over and took my hand. "I'm more concerned about Zoey than Andy right now. She was sobbing."

I glanced at my food. "Could we get to-go containers? I can't eat."

Blake motioned to the server and asked for take-home boxes. We drove back to the office but remained in the car after we parked. "He's bothered that you were in the house for the party and took on the role of his mother."

"Makes sense."

"But it doesn't bother Allison at all. She loves that you're a part of my life."

I placed my hand on his arm. "Allison has had time to process being in the house after Cheryl's death and not having her mother there. This past week was the first time Andy has been back to the house since Cheryl's passing. He saw me as 'the other woman.'" I pulled my hand away and stared out the windshield. "But I have a theory."

"I'd love to hear it." Blake sighed and rubbed his jaw.

~

After lunch, Jocelyn and I interviewed our remaining candidates—Tauni and Terri.

On her way out of the interview, Tauni paused and whispered, "I missed not getting together for lunch with you this week. Are we on for next Wednesday?" Her eyes sparkled. "I have news to share."

Tauni and I had arranged to meet on a weekly basis to chat over lunch. I looked forward to spending time with her and growing our friendship.

"Now I'm curious," I said. "We could meet at our 3:00 break."

"Great. I'll come to your office—more private than my cubicle." She walked away with a bounce in her step.

After our interview with Terri, Jocelyn and I stepped into her office and closed the door. "I don't imagine there's any question. Tauni is the right fit. Agree?" Jocelyn said.

I nodded. "Alicia needs to work full-time and prove herself, even if she is the chairman of the board's niece. Hopefully, Walt will understand. And if Terri feels she needs a change and she accepts, we can move her out of Legal and put her into Tauni's position in the Insurance Department."

Jocelyn agreed. "What do you think about Alicia moving to Legal since Marketing doesn't need her full-time?"

"Might work. Terri will be here to train her, and that's a plus."

We decided to follow-up with Blake and confirm our decision on Monday before we talked with the three candidates.

I peeked at my watch and slipped over to my office at 3:01.

Tauni straightened when I rushed in.

"Well? Don't make me beg?" I rested against the front of my desk. "Have you heard from Quade?"

Tauni slumped in her chair. "How did you know? Did he tell Blake he planned to ask me out?"

"Girl, I saw the same look on your face when you said you had something to tell me that was there when Quade asked you to dance at our party. You've been smitten."

Her eyes grew wide. "Perhaps. But let's keep this between us, okay?"

"You mean I can't tell Blake?"

"Especially not Blake." She shook her head and stood. "I don't want word to get back to Quade."

I hugged her. "Do me a favor." I pulled away. "Go slow. He seems like a personable guy, but . . ."

She smiled. "I understand, and I'm praying the Lord shows me red flags sooner rather than later. I don't want a repeat of my previous relationships." Tauni grinned. "Are the interviews finished?"

"We'll have a decision on Monday. I'll let you know."

She thanked me on her way out.

At 5:00, I hurried to my car. I needed to cook dinner and think through my theory regarding Andy so I could share it with Blake tonight. *Can I explain it without placing the blame on him?*

Six

By the time Blake arrived at my condo, I'd prepared lasagna, made a salad, put garlic bread into the oven and set the table.

"Dinner will be ready in a few minutes." I took his jacket and hung it in the hall closet.

He met me in the kitchen and gazed into my eyes. "I missed you today."

I tilted my head. "You saw me this morning and we ate lunch together."

"But you weren't at your desk when I walked by—the old one or your new one."

"The interviews, remember?" I patted his cheek. "Have a seat at the table."

"How did the interviews go? Do I have a new assistant?"

I placed the lasagna in the center of the table. "They went well. Jocelyn and I agreed that Tauni is the best fit for you." I grabbed the salad and bread and took my seat. "If that's okay with you, I'll talk with her Monday and give her the good news."

"I'd like to be involved in that. Hopefully, she'll suppose I had something to do with the decision. Might be a confidence booster for her. What do you think?"

"A great idea." I held his hand and smiled. "Will you say the blessing?"

After Blake prayed over our meal, he took his first bite of lasagna. "This is good. Almost as good as . . ."

I stared at him with my mouth opened and waited for him to complete his sentence.

He swallowed hard and said. "This is delicious."

"As good as whose? Cheryl's?"

Color rose in his cheeks. "No. Cheryl couldn't boil water. That's why I hired Richard, my chef. He makes a mean lasagna. But yours is *every* bit as good." He grinned.

"Yeah. Like I believe you." I stood and ambled to my refrigerator. "Maybe extra cheese will improve the taste." I brought a bag of shredded mozzarella to the table and dropped it next to Blake's plate.

"K, I'm sorry. My mouth works faster than my brain."

"I'm fine." I crossed my arms. "There must be something I can whip up that you'll like better than Richard's." I didn't hide my irritation.

He offered me his hand. "What's for dessert? I'm sure that will be amazing."

I ignored his hand, took my seat, and smirked. "Ice cream. From the store. Mayfield Creamery makes a mean chocolate almond."

As soon as we finished our meal, Blake rose and gathered our plates. "I'll do the dishes."

Someone feeling guilty?

"You go relax and spend time with Roxie. Does she have other favorite places to perch or only the kitchen counter?"

I put away the rest of the food. "She doesn't do that

often. She's a good kitty." I strolled down the hallway and found Roxie asleep on my bed. "Mommy wants you to meet someone." I picked her up and carried her out to Blake. "Here's my precious baby."

Blake backed away and raised his hands. "I don't like cats."

Annoyed, I said, "I'll finish the dishes later. Go sit down on the sofa, and I'll put her on the floor in front of you. I expect she'll run back down the hallway."

He trudged to the living room and took a seat. Roxie eyed him for a few minutes from her spot on the floor. Blake glanced at her and meowed.

I giggled. "She's entertained by you. She hasn't run off yet."

Roxie leapt into his lap and purred. Blake stiffened, but she didn't mind. She continued to rub her head against his arm, and after a few seconds, she curled up into a ball and closed her eyes.

"You found a new friend."

His voice squeaked. "Take her, please?"

I placed Roxie on the floor and sat next to Blake. "Can we talk about Andy?"

"I'm ready and interested in your theory."

"After Andy told you that he and Zoey planned to move to Nashville, he saw us in the kitchen together. When you gave me the salmon colored rose, he was descending the back stairs." I sighed and clasped Blake's hand. "He darted up the steps when I glanced his way."

"I'm not following why that's important? He saw us together often at the party."

I looked at Roxie, who'd fallen asleep at Blake's feet. "I imagine he heard you tell me I was your one-and-only. To him, it could sound as though I'm more important to you than Cheryl was." I fidgeted to get comfortable. "If this is what he thinks, it's understandable he doesn't want to be here with us. Maybe Andy sees you as a traitor and believes you've betrayed Cheryl's memory."

Blake stood and shook his head. "What do we do now? I won him back and I've lost him again?" He peered at me.

Blake's phone rang, and he removed it from his pocket. "Andy."

His voice rose in volume. "They what? Someone at *our* party? That's ridiculous. You were there the whole time . . . We have witnesses . . ." Blake paced across my living room. "Don't worry about this. You're good . . . Okay, bye."

Blake groaned and took a seat next to me on the sofa. "This is a mess. Who told the police Andy left the party early when we know he was there the entire time?"

"One of our guests said Andy left early?" I narrowed my eyes and frowned.

"They saw him slip out the patio doors around 4:55 p.m. and not return."

"But everyone left around that time. How would they know if or when he returned?"

"Not everyone left. Besides family, three others stayed later."

~

Blake and I both found the information difficult to accept. We had told the police how late everyone stayed that night. Those who left soon after 5:00, which were most of the guests, couldn't expect to know when Andy returned, if he'd gone anywhere. That meant Wes, Tauni, or Walt lied to the police because they all stayed until

6:00.

After we came to that conclusion, Blake suggested we both consider this possibility and talk about it the next day.

Saturday morning, while I prepared breakfast, my phone rang. "Zoey? You're up early. Is everything okay?"

"We fought and he left."

Oh my. I pulled my bacon from the skillet and placed it on a paper towel. "What happened?"

"We argued about moving back to Nashville." She sobbed. "He said it won't ever happen."

"Oh, honey. I'm sure he'll be back. He loves you." I turned off the burner and moved the skillet. "We're the reason you got into a fight, aren't we?"

"He said something about you and his dad, but he won't tell me what happened."

"Blake and I have talked about this, and we may know what's troubling him. I'm sure he and Blake will be able to work this out."

I prayed with Zoey and asked the Lord to fill her with His peace and to bring Andy back soon. "Please call me when you hear from him."

When we ended the call, I clicked on Blake's number.

"Well, good morning. Were you awake thinking about me all night?"

I cleared my throat. "Not quite, but it's a nice thought." I snickered and told him about Zoey's call and their argument. "I guess she suspects he may not return home soon."

"He'll be back. He's crazy about her."

"That's what I told her."

"I'm getting another call, and I'll call you back." He disconnected.

Ten minutes later, my phone rang again. Blake said, "That was Andy."

"Is he back home?"

"Let's meet for breakfast and I'll fill you in—Cracker Barrel near Cool Springs?"

"I'm eating now—bacon and pancakes. Come on over, and I'll prepare more."

Blake arrived twenty minutes later. I'd already fried more bacon and prepared the extra batter. I poured the batter onto the griddle while Blake and I chatted.

"Andy called to verify the detective's phone number so he can call them back. He remembered he carried a bag of garbage out through the great room's patio doors as the party was wrapping up and came back inside through the kitchen. He went upstairs to use the restroom and wouldn't have been seen by anyone for several minutes until he came back downstairs and helped with cleanup."

"That makes sense." I flipped the pancakes and took plates from the cabinet. "What did Andy say about he and Zoey?"

"He said he needed to get away for a few hours. He might spend the night with a friend."

"Do you think he'll call and tell Zoey that's his plan?"

"I encouraged him to do so." Blake jerked. "Yikes. Your monster cat tried to attack me."

I tilted my head back and laughed. "She rubbed her head against your legs and claimed you as her own." I cupped my hand on his cheek and gazed into his eyes. "Like I'm doing now."

"Oh. I assumed that she was saying she wanted me to leave."

I kissed his other cheek and flipped the pancakes. "Now that you've had time to process the information, who do you suppose intended to make Andy look guilty?"

He turned my chin toward him. "I don't judge this as an attack on Andy. Whoever said this about him wants to hurt me."

Seven

While we ate breakfast, we discussed the possibilities. At first, I agreed with Blake that someone wanted to hurt him. But as I considered it more, I decided the entire thing could have been a misunderstanding and told him so.

"Misunderstanding? Keedryn, you're getting soft." He rubbed the back of his neck. "How did you come up with that?"

"Anyone who left the party around 5:00 would have been speaking the truth if they'd seen Andy leave but not return. That person had already gone home by the time Andy went back to the great room to help rearrange the furniture." I stood and snatched our empty plates from the table. I didn't like the way Blake glared at me. "Perhaps they didn't mean to imply anything when they shared that bit of information with the police."

"You can't accept that one of your friends is out to get me, can you? My money's on Wes." Blake got up from his chair and came up behind me while I placed the dishes in the sink. When I turned, he let out a lengthy sigh.

"But why would Wes do that? He's a good man. You've said so yourself."

Blake grasped my hand and led me to the living room. We took seats next to one another on the couch, and he pulled me close. "K, Wes loves you. He's suffering from a broken heart. You dumped him, and jealousy consumes him. He's not thinking well."

I rose and plodded to the kitchen. Annoyed, I raised my voice. "You're not thinking either."

~

Footsteps behind me. *Great, he followed me.* I spun toward him. "How could I dump him if we didn't have a relationship?"

"Your connection was one of friendship that he desired to become much more. Maybe we should call this unrequited love." Blake stepped closer and laid his hands on my shoulders. "Watch him. He may turn on you too. Let me know if he becomes manipulative or pushy." Blake caressed my hair.

I took a step back. "Walt's to blame. I've never trusted him." *The way he's eyed me in the past.* I shuddered at the thought.

Blake chuckled. "Why would Walt want to hurt me? He's a friend."

I straightened and looked Blake in the eye. "And Wes is my friend. He knows if he hurt you, he'd hurt me too."

"Okay. That leaves Tauni. She wants to bring us both down—her future supervisor and her current friend and mentor." He laughed again and shook his head.

"You're making a joke about this. I'm sticking with the idea that the entire thing was a misunderstanding."

"Sure." He placed his hands on my arms. "But if either of us experiences anything unusual from any of the three in question, we'll tell one another everything.

Deal?"

I sighed and nodded. *I'll tell you if I don't think you'll get angry with me.*

~

Blake finished tidying up my kitchen and told me that he had a surprise for me. A quick trip to Franklin. He didn't tell me his plans but said we'd spend time outdoors and to wear a coat. Twenty minutes later, when he pulled into a car dealership, I squealed and bounced in my seat.

Blake cut me a look. "For someone who didn't want a new car, you seem giddy."

I clapped in rapid succession. "I guess I am excited."

He told me if I wanted a red Escape, we'd need to special order one which could take a few weeks. But if I wanted a blue one, I could take it today, or I could have a red Edge—a larger vehicle. After we looked at both, I stayed with the Escape and took the blue one. Blake traded in his BMW, and I drove us to his house.

After I parked in front of his home and climbed out, I dashed to the passenger side and kissed his cheek. "Thank you. I love this car." I gazed into his eyes. "Is that a tear in your eye? Are you mourning the loss of your BMW?"

"Allergies."

"But it's the middle of winter. Oh, Blake. You're not allergic to cats, are you?"

He laughed. "I should tell you yes, so you don't bring that monster into my home. But no, new cars always cause me trouble until I air them out for a week. I'm fine." He held my hand and led me toward his front door.

"I should go. I need to stop by Jenny's and show her

my new wheels."

"After another jaunt. For this one, we need my pickup."

"Where?"

"Another surprise. I imagine you'll react differently than you did at the car lot, though."

~

We traveled south again, toward Franklin, but we were out in the country. Beautiful farmland. Blake turned down a dirt road. We drove for a mile before he took a gravel driveway. He stopped at the top of a hill that overlooked a pond. The rolling meadows reminded me of a painting in his office, except there weren't any cows grazing.

"Beautiful," I said. "Where are we?"

"I'll come around to help you out. I want you to meet Sonny." He opened my door, grasped my hand, and turned me around toward a young man who strutted our way.

"Is that Sonny?" As he got closer, I realized it was Quade, perhaps Tauni's new beau whom I'd met at our party. "So good to see you again." I stuck out my hand to shake his. "You have a wonderful place here."

"Ma'am. Good to see you too." After he shook my hand, he gaped at Blake. "Something you want to tell me, boss? Are you deeding the place to me?" Quade grinned and crossed his arms.

"Boss?" I peered at them both. "Is this land yours, Blake?"

"Quade's my ranch manager. I own all you see here, but he runs the place."

I ambled to the front of the pickup and stared out toward the tree line. "Where's the property line? How large is your ranch?"

Blake took my hand again and pointed. "Two hundred acres. Past the tree line. Would you like to see more?"

"Yes." He'd never told me about his ranch. "But how can you afford all of this?"

He chuckled. "Remember when I told you that my uncle made his fortune in the music business? And how part of his estate assists young people getting started in both Christian and country music?"

"And you make those disbursement decisions now on his behalf."

"He never married or had children of his own. So, because of our close relationship, he left me his entire estate when he died ten years ago. This ranch and my home belonged to him."

"Had you spent much time here before it became yours?" I released Blake's hand, pulled my gloves out of my pockets, and put them on.

"See that cabin across the way?" He pointed to a log cabin. "My second home. My uncle taught me to fish, hunt, and raise cattle. We had some great summers together here."

Blake glanced back at Quade and strode toward him.

I slipped in closer to hear.

Blake said, "Are you kidding? You're perfect for her. What do you have planned?"

I smiled. "Are we talking about Tauni?"

Quade's face turned red. "You're friends, right?"

"Yes, we are."

He brushed his boot across the gravel.

"I'm happy you asked her out," I said. "The two of you appeared to hit it off well at our party."

He grinned and thanked me.

"So, where's this Sonny you want me to meet?" I squinted at Blake.

Quade whistled and a beautiful, medium-sized, fluffy dog ran toward us. When she came to me, her whole back side wriggled. If she'd had a tail, it would have swished back and forth. I knelt and buried my face into her black, white, and tan fur.

"K, are you okay?"

I looked up at Blake. "We had an Australian Shepherd at my grandparents' farm." I rubbed Sonny behind her ears and stood. "What's next. I need to see more of the ranch now before I kidnap her."

Sonny followed Quade as he headed toward the cabin, which sat on the edge of the property, and Blake and I climbed into the truck. He drove to another hill and parked. The pond glimmered in the sunlight when I glanced back toward where we met Quade and Sonny.

"This is another lovely spot," I said.

Blake turned me in the other direction and pointed. "Do you see them?"

I placed my hand above my eyes to block the sun. "Cattle. How many do you own?"

"I have one hundred and Quade owns thirty."

"My grandparents raised cattle. And chickens. Do you have chickens?" I turned my head away from Blake. I didn't realize this road trip would be such an emotional time for me.

"No." He moved in front of me and lifted my chin. "I thought bringing you out here might stir your emotions, but not because of the cows. I'm afraid to take you to our third and final stop."

"Why?" I tilted my head. "What's next?"

"Hop in."

We drove a little farther back on the property to a field that must be amazing in the springtime. Because it was beautiful in winter with brown grass and bare trees. To the right of where we parked flowed a meandering stream along the tree line, and to the left . . . a lonely twisted tree with gnarled branches—a tree for climbing—if I were a younger woman. A tree like the one where I'd found my Savior thirty-some years earlier.

I climbed out of the truck and faced the stream. "This is the exact view from the painting in your office. Did Cheryl paint that one?"

"Cheryl didn't like the ranch. She seldom came out here. I took a photo and hired an artist to paint it for me." He placed his arm around my shoulder. "I've seen you stare at the painting in my office and suspected you might like this spot the best. Am I right?"

"This is my favorite." *But not because of the stream or the painting. The tree—another tree of life.* I needed to keep my love for the tree a secret. Blake would assume that I was a nutty woman for sure if I told him why this was my favorite spot.

"I suppose this will work well." He smirked and enveloped me in a tight embrace.

"What will work well?"

"Your surprise."

I took a step back and peered into his eyes. "I thought showing me the ranch *was* my surprise."

He rubbed his palms together and placed them on both sides of my face. "Your cheeks are red. Let's get you inside the truck." He escorted me to the passenger door, and I climbed in. Inside, he grabbed a folder from the back seat and handed it to me.

I scrunched up my face and glanced at him. "This *is* a marvelous surprise. You want me to work today?"

He pointed to the folder. "Open it."

I lifted the cover and stared at the contents—house plans. Several of them.

Blake laid his hand on top of mine. "I want us to have *our place*. A home we both enjoy—a house where we can grow old together." He brought my hand to his lips and kissed my fingers. "Do you think you could be happy here on the ranch with me?"

I gazed into his eyes. "You'd give up your mansion for me?"

"I'd do anything for you, K. And I'm willing to give up my house for us. We don't need that many rooms."

Blake knew I didn't like his enormous home. I told him two months before, that I'd rather live in something much smaller.

I blinked several times and looked at the photos. "Let's go back to my place. I'll fix us lunch, and we can pour over these house plans."

"Instead, I'll take you back to my place, and you can get your car. You look over the plans and pick out your favorites and we'll go from there. I've reviewed all of them, and any will do. You decide. If you don't see what you want and need, we'll keep looking."

I hugged his neck. My lips moved from his cheek to his lips before we backed away from our parking spot and drove down the long driveway to the road.

Eight

Too excited to review the plans, I didn't want to take time to fix lunch. I used the drive-through at Chick-fil-A instead. When I arrived home, I spread out the plans on my kitchen counter to sort them into one-story and two-story groups. No need. They were all two. I searched for those with a master bedroom downstairs and found three. But when I scanned the details, they were all over 5,000 square feet—one as much as 8,000. Why did two people need such a large home?

Blake told me that his mansion was about 10,000 square feet, so I was happy these were smaller, but not small enough. I didn't want to complain, but because we wouldn't have children living with us, 2,000 would make me happier. I shuffled the plans together and stared at them. *What do I do now? He's giving up the house he and Cheryl shared for several years, and I'm still not happy. What's wrong with me?*

My phone pinged with a text: Have you reviewed the plans, or are you showing off your new car to Jenny?

Jenny? I snatched my coat and the plans and hurried outside. Jenny would love to see the house plans and my car.

I sent Blake a text: Leaving to visit Jenny now. Call

you soon.

When Carl opened the front door, he stepped aside for me to enter, but he left the door open. "You bought a new car?"

Jenny and Nicki scurried down the hallway toward me.

Often, Nicki stops to hug her nana, but she ran past me to the door. "I want to see too."

"Mom, it's beautiful. Why didn't you tell me that you planned to get a new car? I would have helped you pick one. Did Blake go with you?" Jenny grabbed their coats from the hall closet and all four of us went outside for a closer look.

"Blake bought it for me."

Jenny waggled her eyebrows. "You got yourself a keeper—and I don't mean the car." She closed the driver's door that Carl had opened. "A beautiful necklace and now a car. What's next?"

I lifted the folder. "These. Blake helped me pick out the car, but I need your help to pick out a house."

"He plans to sell his mansion? Don't you want to live there?"

"I don't. He has a ranch that reminds me of my grandparents' farm. He wants to have a house built there for us. As he put it, 'our place.'"

She took the folder out of my hands. "Well then, let's look." She jogged to the door and rushed inside.

"Wait." Carl sounded anxious. "Your new car is blocking mine in the garage. Jenny's craving chocolate. I need to pick some up for her at the convenience store."

I tossed Carl my keys. "Take my car."

"Great. I'll be back in ten minutes."

Nicki and I followed Jenny into the house and found

her at the kitchen counter.

"Blake's sweet to do this for me, but they're all too big. What should I do?"

Jenny sorted through the plans and put them in order by size. "We have four under 6,000 square feet." Do you like any of these?" She slid them my way.

"I'd prefer a bedroom downstairs. Only two of these have one. When we get older, we may have a hard time with the steps." I studied both plans and handed one to Jenny. "This one seems more like a ranch house than the other. But it's too big."

"Mom. You may need to compromise on this. Look, a great room, sunroom, formal dining, and master suite with a master study. Nice. And look at this veranda along the back."

"Yes, but there's only room for three cars. We'll have four."

"Blake has three of his own?"

"He had four until he traded in his BMW for my Escape." I told her about his pickup and the Infiniti SUV he bought me and how I didn't want it. I slumped in my chair. "Oh, no. I don't dare complain about the size of the house too."

While I was telling her about the Ferrari, Carl walked in and said, "Ferrari? Do you think Blake will let me take that for a spin?"

I chuckled and shrugged. "I'm not asking him for you."

"Let's look at the second floor." Jenny tapped her finger on the house plan. She sounded eager to check every detail.

I returned my attention to her and the second floor. "Three more bedrooms with private bathrooms for guests, a recreation room, and a viewing deck off the front and back."

"And look at the bonus room on the third level with eight dormer windows all the way around." Jenny opened her eyes wide.

"I must admit, it's an amazing house. And the spot where we plan to build is beautiful too."

Carl joined us at the table and scanned the plan. "Only 5,500 square feet. That's a lot smaller than what Blake has now."

"Yes, he's cutting back to half its size for me."

"Half? Don't you mean a third?"

"What?"

"Jim told me Blake's house is over 15,000 square feet."

I stared at Carl with my mouth opened. *That can't be right. He told me 10,000. Didn't he? Back in November?*

"Let's go see it and Papa Blake." Nicki jumped up and down.

~

When I called Blake and told him I'd selected a house, he said he'd pick me up for dinner to celebrate. He mentioned a few other things we needed to discuss. And I wanted to discuss something with him—15,000 square feet.

By the time he arrived, I'd changed and freshened up. With the house plan stuck in my purse, I stepped outside before he rang my doorbell.

He took a step back off my porch. "I love how you can't wait to see me." He escorted me to his car and opened the passenger door. "My darling."

I shook my head and climbed inside. "I think it's you

who enjoys being with me."

"You got that right, sweetheart."

"Darling? Sweetheart? What did you do now?" I glanced into the back seat to find out if another gift awaited me.

"I'm trying out little pet names or nicknames for you. Do you prefer anything in particular?" We pulled out onto the road in front of my condo and headed north.

"You already gave me one—K."

"Need something else like cutie pie."

"Why, so after you've caused trouble you can use your pet name for me to get back on my good side?"

He grinned. "Will any of those work?"

"No. What about peaches?"

"Allergic." He chuckled. "Precious?"

"Let's table this topic for now. What did you want to discuss?"

He reached over and caressed my cheek. "First, did you hear from Zoey?"

"No. I'll text her." I pulled out my phone and typed: **Did Andy get home okay?** "I hope she'll respond soon."

"Me too. I'm concerned about them both." Blake turned and parked at a local steakhouse. "Great steaks here. Sound good to you?"

"Sure."

During our thirty-minute wait for a table, I pulled out the house plan. "This house won't be too small for you, will it?" I handed the paper to Blake. "Only *half* the size of what you're accustomed to?"

His eyes darted from me to the sheet of paper he held in his hands and back to me. He furrowed his brows. "About that. My house is around 15,000 square feet, not the 10,000 I first implied." His shoulders drooped and he frowned. "I'm cutting way back for you. Is this still too big?"

"I think we can make it work, but I need you to be upfront with me. About everything."

"I'm sorry, K. You were so adamant about Walt's house being too big that day we went there for the finance meeting. I didn't want to scare you off over the size of my house." He pulled me close and scanned the plan I'd given him and agreed with my choice. He said the builder was ready to get started, and we should move into our new home by the end of October.

We sat across from one another in a booth, placed our order, and chatted until our food arrived.

After the waitress delivered our food, Blake offered a sweet prayer of thanksgiving. "I have a couple of things to talk with you about."

"And they are. . .?"

"My estate plan."

I choked on my baked potato and coughed. "What?"

"While I was on the phone with my attorney, we talked about changing it. Do you have a will?"

"I do, but I haven't updated it since Sam's death."

"Let's go visit Matt together and get that taken care of. He wants to review the changes to mine, and we can get his advice on yours too."

I was at a loss for words and glanced around the restaurant. "Is that necessary?"

"Yes, it is." He reached over and touched my hand again. "I plan to take care of you. You need to know the details of my estate plan."

"But your children come first. And besides, we're not married yet. Can't we do this after our wedding?"

He gazed at the ceiling and back at me. "I'd like to

take care of it now while it's fresh on my mind. I made us an appointment for Monday afternoon. Does that work for you?"

I rolled my eyes and took a sip of water. "Whatever."

"Great." He leaned back and smiled. "Now. Let's talk about Aunt Mary."

This time I choked on my steak. "Is your goal to kill me tonight?"

He put his hand over his mouth to muffle his laugh. "I should have waited until you swallowed, pumpkin."

"No. Pumpkin won't work." I lifted my palm toward Blake. "My dad and grandpa called me that."

"What did your Aunt Mary call you?"

"K." I peered into his eyes.

His smile faded, and he rubbed the back of his neck. "Honey, I feel terrible. I've called you K for months and you never told me." He left his side of the booth and came over to my side with his plate of food. He wrapped his arm around me and held me close.

"Blake, it's okay. I realized that when you said it, you used it as an endearment. She used it to annoy me." I pulled away to see his entire face and grinned. "I love the way you say K."

He cut another bite of steak. "But it sounds like you need to be upfront with me too."

"Okay." I rested my head on his shoulder. "But honey won't work either. I don't care for the stuff."

He chuckled and said he'd keep trying. "Where does your aunt live?"

"South of Tampa, with my cousin, Vivian." I straightened and picked up my fork.

"Tampa? How long has it been since you visited

her?"

"Do we *have* to talk about this?" I looked up at him and tilted my head.

"Please? I want to know more about your relationship with her." He took a long drink of water. "When was the last time you saw your aunt?"

I glanced at my food. *He'll think I'm a terrible person.* I whispered, "Thirty years."

He raised his eyebrows. "Really? Thirty years? When was the last time you talked on the phone?"

I put my fork down and scooted away from him. My voice squeaked. "Thirty years."

"Email? Text?"

I shook my head.

Blake stared at me. "I think it's time to pay Aunt Mary a visit. I'll go with you. And you can meet my Mom. She lives in Tampa too." He reached for my hand.

I scooted as far away as possible—an entire eight inches. I sat between a wall and a monster. With as much sternness as I could muster, I said, "Not happening."

Nine

On our drive back to my place, I stared straight ahead and didn't say a word. I didn't care what he wanted. I would not allow him to coerce me into visiting my aunt. For God to get my attention on this, He'd need to speak in an audible voice and knock me on the head with something. There was no reason to visit that woman.

I didn't wait for Blake to turn off the ignition when he pulled into a parking space. I jumped out of his car and hurried to my door.

"K. Wait."

I spun toward him and pointed my index finger in his face. Bitterness oozed from my lips. "No, you wait. Drop the topic now or don't come back until you're ready to end this ridiculous conversation. And let me repeat what I said earlier." I clenched my jaw. "Not happening."

Blake took a step back and lifted his palms toward me. "I guess I'll see you Monday at the office." He turned and strode to his car. He didn't sound upset. Just walked away.

I entered my condo, shut the front door, and trudged to my bedroom. After I threw my purse across the room,

I flung myself onto my bed. "I will not visit that horrible woman. I won't."

~

On Sunday morning, I couldn't bring myself to go to church. I knew I acted like a child. A spoiled brat kind of child. Church was where I needed to be, but I struggled to make myself go.

I prepared peppermint tea and gazed out my kitchen window to my tiny back yard. *Lord, please don't ask me to visit Aunt Mary. Not now. Not after so many years.* I should have gone long ago when I forgave her. *Forgave her?* Would I have acted like a child last night if I'd forgiven her? Yes, I forgave her. But that didn't mean I must accept her back into my life. *Right, Lord?*

I plodded to my bedroom to get my phone from my purse. The purse I threw across the room the night before. *What's wrong with me? When was the last time I got so upset?* I don't throw things. I sighed and glanced in my full-length mirror. *Yikes, Keedryn. You look as terrible as you feel.* With hair matted around my face and my dark eyes, I might frighten a child. Glad Nicki couldn't see me.

With my phone in hand, I padded back to my kitchen and took a seat at the table. I clicked on Blake's number and waited through four rings. He sounded irritated when he answered. I couldn't blame him because I was frustrated with myself.

"I'm sorry for the way I acted. Thought I forgave her years ago, but I guess that's not the case. . . Blake?"

"Are you ready to talk now?"

"About anything except Aunt Mary."

"I'm headed out to the ranch to help Quade today. I'll see you tomorrow at the office. Maybe we can do lunch—*if* you're ready to talk about your Aunt Mary."

He hung up, expressing no plans to back down. What right did he have to take such a strong stand? None. I could be just as stubborn. *You wait Blake. You'll see how stubborn I can be.*

~

After I showered and dressed, I received a text from Zoey: Andy's home. No to Nashville.

I copied Zoey's text, sent it to Blake, and responded to her: I let Blake know. Praying for you both. Miss you.

I ate a bowl of cereal and made a batch of chocolate chip cookies. While the cookies baked, I prayed for Andy and Zoey, but my stomach ached over Blake and his insistence I visit my aunt. I opened my Bible and read chapter three of Colossians.

Verse thirteen got my attention. "Bear with each other and forgive one another if any of you has a grievance against someone. Forgive as the Lord forgave you." Grievance? She wronged me—treated me like scum when I was a kid. *Yes, that word fits. But I have forgiven. Why is the thought of a visit with her so difficult for me?*

I sensed the Lord prompting me to surrender my grievance to Him and forgive again because of the resentment that had grown in my heart. I knelt on my kitchen floor.

When I finished, one problem remained. Although I gave my grievance to the Lord and forgave my aunt— again—I struggled with Blake's pushing me to visit her. Why was it so important to him?

~

At the office on Monday morning, I fixed Blake a cup of coffee and placed it on his desk to get back on his good side. I expected he'd arrive before it got cold.

I went to my office and met with Jocelyn to verify she wanted to move ahead with Tauni's promotion to executive assistant. When she confirmed, I scheduled time in the morning to meet with Tauni first and follow up with Alicia and Terri to give them news of our decision.

My desk phone rang. Blake. After I greeted him, he asked, "Are we having lunch together today?"

I sighed and closed my eyes. "No. Won't work for me." I still didn't want to discuss my aunt.

"Okay. Thank you for the coffee." I heard the shuffle of papers. "I'll call and cancel our meeting with my attorney this afternoon."

What? "Cancel?"

"Postpone. We're under enough stress right now without adding other decisions into the mix." He paused for several seconds. "I love you."

"And I you." We disconnected the call.

When Tauni arrived for her appointment, I remembered that Blake wanted to be present when we told her we chose her for the coveted position.

"I'll be right back." I rose when she sat, scooted down the hall, and hurried into Blake's office. "Excuse me. But I forgot to send you a meeting request to meet with Tauni and me. Are you available? She's in my office."

He stood. "Thank you for including me now."

We walked down the hall together. In my office, he greeted Tauni and sat next to her. I took a seat at my desk.

I nodded at Blake for him to take the lead.

He turned toward Tauni. "Although I wasn't present for your interview, Keedryn tells me that you aced it.

Congratulations. If you want the position, it's yours."

She clapped, stood, and took a step toward Blake. She stopped herself before she hugged him. "Oops." She stepped back and turned bright red.

Blake pointed at me. "She'll take my hugs for me." He smiled at Tauni, looked at me, and slipped out the door.

Tauni ran around my desk and embraced me. "Thank you so much. I'll make you proud, and I won't disappoint either you or Blake with your decision."

"I know you'll do a superb job. Blake knows it too."

My meetings with Terri and Alicia went well. They were both disappointed that they weren't chosen, but they were happy with their pending moves. We needed their manager's approval before we proceeded with their transfers and training.

Blake called me at 11:00. "Do you have time to review letters for me and prepare a spreadsheet? I need them by 4:00 today."

"Sure. Send me the links."

He spoke in a soft tone. "Could you come to my office for a few minutes?"

"I'll be right there."

We sat at his conference table next to one another. "I need to take a day off to travel." He glanced toward his office door and back at me. "I'd like you to come with me."

"To visit Andy and Zoey?"

"Later. But this week I need to visit my mother."

"Your mother?" I jumped up. "Like I believe you." I knew where this was going.

"No tricks. I won't insist on your visiting your aunt while we're there, although I think you should. But Mom would like to meet you before the wedding."

I returned to my seat. "You're backing down? Not demanding I *must* visit Aunt Mary?"

"K, I don't want to fight. I shouldn't have insisted. Your decision, not mine."

"Thank you." I gripped his hand underneath the table. "That means a lot to me. I'll ask the Lord again what He wants me to do." I tilted my head. "Why did you push me so hard on this?"

"My sister hasn't spoken to me in ten years. I've tried. Flew to Europe to talk with her, but she didn't want me there."

I squeezed his hand and offered my full attention.

"I feel strongly that you need to at least try to make amends with your aunt. This may be your last opportunity." He stared over the top of my head. "Besides, families shouldn't fight. If things don't work out, then nothing's lost. But something great could come out of it."

"Ten years? Your uncle's estate?"

He nodded. "Lydia and I developed a close relationship as kids and remained close during adulthood. She should have known I'd be fair with her." He dropped his head and closed his eyes. "But when I tried to work things out early on, she was too mad at the world. She despises me, even though I've tried several times since then to make this right."

I pulled my hand away from his and rubbed his arm. "I'd love to meet your mom, but I don't think it will be proper for us to travel alone together."

He frowned. "Somehow I knew you'd say that. We traveled to Albuquerque and that was okay, but this isn't?"

"I traveled as your executive assistant. This time I'll travel as your fiancée."

"And that's why Allison offered to go with us." He smirked. "To chaperone."

"Fantastic. I'll love having her along." I grinned. "Do you still want to have lunch together?"

He stood. "I thought I'd like to take my new assistant to lunch."

"Oh?" I widened my eyes.

"To celebrate. But I'd prefer you join us. Agree?"

I confirmed and called Tauni.

We met in the lobby at 11:30 and proceeded to the parking lot.

Tauni scanned the area. "I don't see either of your cars. Did you jog to work this morning?"

Blake glanced around, stopped walking, and pointed at a Harley-Davidson. "We came in together on the bike. Do you think there's room for three?"

I shook my head and looked at Tauni. "I'll pray for you every day to endure his weird sense of humor and moods."

She chuckled.

I stepped over to my new car. "This is mine." Blake's new Infiniti was parked next to my Escape with the driver's side facing us. "This is Blake's."

"Nice. I like them both." Tauni hurried to the passenger side of the Infiniti, gasped, and placed her hand over her chest.

I dashed over next to her and groaned.

Blake bounded toward us and almost swore, but he caught himself. He darted from the back bumper to the front headlight. "Two lines the entire side of my car. This wasn't an accident. Someone keyed my Infiniti." He ran his hand through his hair. "Maybe now they'll listen to me. I told the executive team months ago we need security cameras out here."

Tauni and I gawked at the damage.

"Who would do this?" Blake took out his cell and dialed. "I'd like to report vandalism on my new car." He moved away from us and turned his back. After he put his cell into his pocket, he walked up next to me. "I'll wait here for an officer to arrive. You can have lunch without me."

I touched his arm. "I'm sorry this happened."

He pushed past me with his eyes down and stared at the damage. "We'll talk about it later."

Ten

Tauni and I lunched at a local hamburger place. She waited until we placed our order to tell me what I was dying to know. She scooted closer to the table where we sat across from one another. "Quade and I enjoy each other's company. He's such a gentleman and kind."

"And?" I opened my eyes wide.

"And? Are you asking if he kissed me?"

"That too. But I want to find out when your next date will be."

She stared over my head and grinned. "He kissed me on the cheek when he took me home Saturday evening." Her face glowed. "We attended his church yesterday and spent the afternoon together. He plans to attend my church next weekend."

"I'm glad you're happy. He seems like a great guy, although I don't know him well."

Tauni smiled and peered at me. "I've thought I found the right man before. But it's turned out awful. This is different. Quade's husband material." She wiggled back in her chair and gazed across the restaurant.

"How do you feel about being a rancher's wife?"

"Frightened of something I understand nothing about. But if God's in it, He'll take care of me. I'll trust Him. Although I realize it's too soon to consider ranch life."

I ordered a sandwich for Blake in case he didn't have time to stop for lunch. After we gobbled our burgers, we drove back to the office.

Blake made his way down the hall thirty minutes later and stopped by my desk. "I filed the report and sent pictures off to the insurance company." He huffed and closed my office door. "What a mess. Although I have insurance, the deductible will cost me $1,000." He plopped into a chair and rubbed his chin.

"What are you thinking? You must have an opinion regarding what happened."

"Do I need to tell you who I presume is responsible?"

I rose and closed the door between my office and Jocelyn's that we often kept ajar. "Wes wouldn't do that. Perhaps whoever did isn't acquainted with you. They saw a new car and out of envy they vandalized it."

Blake seethed sarcasm. "And it wasn't Tauni. Must be Walt, although he doesn't know I bought a new car."

"But neither Wes nor Tauni knew that either unless they saw you get out of your car this morning. And Tauni seemed baffled when she looked for our cars in the parking lot." I leaned toward Blake. "I don't imagine Walt did this either. The chance he was here this morning is slim." I tilted my head. "Unless he visited Chad."

Blake stood. "I'll check with Chad before I get back to work. Perhaps you implicated Wes, too." He strode away from my desk.

Thankful I'd left a note in his office earlier and told

him that his lunch was in the employee breakroom refrigerator. I didn't want to say any more to him than needed.

Wes didn't do it. He couldn't have.

~

My afternoon flew by. I stopped in to visit Beth and told her about Blake's car and our discussion over Wes.

"But Wes wouldn't do that." Beth pointed to her extra chair and I took a seat. "He's an exceptional guy."

"That's what I told Blake, but he insists I'm wrong." I crossed my legs and my arms. "Seems we've argued a lot lately."

"Everything will work out. You're stressed right now over learning a new job and planning a wedding. Those are enormous events all by themselves."

I nodded. "Time to get back to work." I said goodbye and hurried back to my office.

After I finished Blake's tasks, I walked down the hall to tell him they were ready and to invite him to dinner. I expected by now he realized his mistake and no longer thought Wes was involved. I entered his office and stood in front of his desk. "Are you feeling better this afternoon?"

He looked up and sighed. "I don't know. I'm frustrated because of the damage and bewildered that you can't see what's happening. This has Wes written all over it." He placed his elbow on his desk with his forehead on his palm.

I stepped backward toward his office door. "No. You're wrong."

He stood. "But it couldn't have been Walt. Chad said Walt and his wife are in Paris."

I turned away, rushed back to my office, and sent

Blake an email to let him know I'd finished his letters and spreadsheet. *Forget dinner tonight. I don't want to be around him.*

~

That evening, after a quick meal, I called Jenny but planned to first talk to Nicki. She possessed a way of cheering me up. "Hi, Nana. I miss you. You don't come see me much anymore."

"Your Papa Blake takes a lot of my time. I'll ask your mama if I can stop by on my way home from work tomorrow. Maybe we can go out to dinner together."

"Yay. Here's Mama now." Nicki told Jenny that she had a date with Nana.

"She's sure excited about getting together with you." Jenny moved to a quieter location. Nicki must have been watching Sesame Street. I heard Cookie Monster in the background.

"I could use your shoulder. Can Carl look after Nicki while you and I meet for coffee or ice cream?"

"Blake trouble?"

"Seems like one thing after another with him."

"If you have chocolate chip cookies, your place sounds wonderful to me."

"Come on over whenever you can."

We disconnected, and I spent the next hour tidying up and praying for the Lord's guidance.

When Jenny arrived, we took our seats next to one another at my kitchen table, ate cookies, and drank hot tea.

"What's up with Blake?" Jenny patted my hand.

I told her about our major arguments—no wedding date, Andy and Zoey problems, Blake's intolerance to cats, someone implicated Andy, and how we disagreed on whom. When I told her that he wanted me to meet his mom and visit Aunt Mary this weekend in Tampa, she stared at me with her mouth opened.

"Does he think you're Wonder Woman? Meet his mom for the first time and come face to face with the woman who terrorized you as a kid all in the same trip?" She pinched her eyebrows together. "That's cruel."

I stood and paced across my kitchen. After I told her how Blake blamed Wes for the vandalism to his new car, I let out a lengthy breath and returned to my seat. "All of this happened in five days."

Jenny reached over, touched my hand, and spoke in a soothing tone. "But he bought you a beautiful necklace, a new car, and plans to build you a house he let you pick out. That says something about your relationship."

"Yes. The man has money. Have you ever known that to impress me?"

"No. But I have one question for you." She narrowed her eyes. "Do you love him?"

"Yes, but we've spent a lot of time together at the office and see each other in the evenings and on weekends. That's my fault. I went into Jocelyn's office on Friday to tell her I couldn't take the HR position and instead I told her yes." I gazed at the ceiling. "Will our married life include so many problems and disagreements?"

"Mom, I will do what you've done with me more than once." She reached for both of my hands and held them in hers. She asked for guidance regarding a visit with Aunt Mary along with wisdom and clarity about the vandalism. And she prayed for Andy and Zoey to work things out between them and for Blake and me to come together as one in unity with the Lord.

"That was beautiful, Jenny." I rose and hugged her neck.

"While I prayed, a thought came to me." She wrinkled her nose. "You may not like it, but I sensed now's the time for you to visit Aunt Mary. I'd love to meet her, too, and be there to support you, if you follow through with a visit."

"Really?"

She stood. "I suppose it's time. She's getting older and not in good health."

My voice wavered. "And how do you know about her health?"

"Aunt Viv and I talk now and then."

I glared at Jenny.

"She told me before Christmas that your aunt wasn't doing well."

She'd been talking with my sis, my cousin by birth, about my aunt? "I can't believe you've talked to Vivian and haven't said a word to me. Did you feel you needed to sneak behind my back?"

She looked me in the eye. "I'm no sneak." She crossed her arms. "Aunt Viv and I like to catch up." She shook her head. "Mom, you do tend to be unreasonable at times. Maybe you should at least try to make amends."

"No promises." I placed my hands on my hips. "Blake plans to leave on Friday and spend the weekend."

Jenny turned and hurried to the door. With her back to me, she said, "Let me know what you decide."

I retired to my bedroom with my Bible and journal. Time to get alone with God.

~

The next morning, a Tuesday, I arrived at the office early with a cup of Starbucks coffee for Blake and three of my homemade chocolate chip cookies. I left them on his desk with an "I love you" note.

A few minutes later, Blake poked his head inside my office. "I'm ready to call a truce. You may be right about Wes. I shouldn't have jumped to conclusions." He took a few steps inside. "Do you have any more of those cookies? Delicious."

"Do you believe what you said about calling a truce? Or are you hoping to get more cookies?"

"I debated about the matter last night. The cookies confirmed I may have been a little hasty." His eyes sparkled. "So, should I order you a ticket to Tampa?"

I inhaled a deep breath and exhaled slowly. "Jenny hopes to join us. Is that possible?"

"Does she want to meet my mom or get away for the weekend?"

"Neither. She wants to meet Aunt Mary."

Eleven

On Thursday morning at break, Tauni stopped by my office and we strolled to the breakroom. She told me that she and Quade ate dinner together twice during the week. He'd also invited her to the ranch Tuesday during lunch and showed her my new home location.

"I love the view near the stream." She poured herself a cup of coffee. "I'll bet it's beautiful in the spring and fall."

"Did you notice the lone tree out in the field?"

"A real eyesore, isn't it?"

I jerked my head back and wrinkled my forehead. "Do you think so? I love that tree."

She gaped at me. "Why?"

I explained my years on my grandparents' farm and how a similar tree became my refuge during hard times.

She placed her free hand on my shoulder and spoke in a melodramatic tone. "That makes it one of the loveliest trees I have ever seen."

I laughed at the theatrical flair in her voice. "You, my dear, are a ham."

"I'm sorry I thought your tree was a dud." She moseyed toward the door. "I need to get back to work.

I'm making lots of notes for Terri when she transfers in next week." She hurried into the hallway.

I worked in a rush all morning and afternoon to make sure I got everything caught up before my trip to Tampa the following day. Jenny shared her excitement that she'd be with me and supporting me when I saw my aunt for the first time in thirty years. She felt awkward about meeting Blake's mom, but Blake assured Jenny that his mom would welcome her.

After I checked in with Terri and Alicia regarding their transfers on Monday, I took the stairs back up to my office and met Wes on his way down.

He smiled and dipped his head. "Nice to see you. You look lovely today in your red blouse. That's a beautiful color on you."

We both stopped, he two steps above me. I glanced up. "Thank you, Wes. Have you had a pleasant week?"

"I've been busy." He descended a step. "I left something on your desk for Nicki." He beamed.

"Which desk? I moved to HR."

"Oh. I left it on your old desk." He walked past me on his way down the stairs.

Something for Nicki? And was he being flirty with me by telling me I looked lovely?

I ambled down the hall to my former office. Blake stood in front of my old desk and held a beautifully wrapped gift. "Is this for you?"

I reached for the package—a small square box, eight inches by eight inches. "A gift for Nicki from Wes. He told me when I met him in the stairway that he left something for her." I stared at the package and pondered what this meant.

"Are you okay?"

I looked up at Blake. "Sure."

Back at my desk with only thirty minutes left before quitting time, I checked my email. I received one from Robin, the administrative assistant who'd taken my place in IT when I became Blake's assistant. "May I meet with you tomorrow? I have a problem with a teammate but don't feel comfortable enough to talk with my manager."

In my reply I told Robin I would be out the following day, but Jocelyn could meet with her. Or if she wanted to wait until Monday, I could meet with her then at 8:30 a.m. She agreed to wait.

After I turned off my computer at 5:00, I strolled down the hall to see Blake. "I'm ready to go home and pack for our trip. I'll see you in the morning around 6:45 a.m."

He stood. "I'm praying for you. You're doing the right thing."

"Am I? By visiting my aunt?"

He stepped around his desk. "Yes. You are."

"I hope so. This may be the hardest conversation I've ever had with someone."

He rubbed his hands up and down my arms. "Have you talked to Vivian?"

"No. I'll feel like I can't change my mind if she knows our plans." I turned to leave and glanced over my shoulder at Blake. "I'll call her when we get to Florida."

~

That evening, when I knelt at the foot of my bed, I focused on my trip. Anxiety flared its ugly head. I hadn't allowed myself to become nervous about meeting Blake's mom for the first time. But seeing Aunt Mary again could be a nightmare.

Would my aunt find fault in everything I said and

did? What if she chastises me for wanting to remarry? Worse, would she dare say something humiliating or cruel to my Jenny?

I poured out my heart to the Lord until peace came, or was it because I grew tired and mistook it for peace? Confusion regarding the visit and what my future held with Blake taunted me.

I padded to my living room and saw the gift for Nicki. A few days without Blake accusing Wes had been good. But doubts clouded my thinking regarding Wes too. I picked up the gift from where I'd placed it on top of my coffee table in the living room. Although I couldn't grasp the thought Wes might be the one who lied to the police or vandalized Blake's car, his gift made me feel uneasy. I carried it to my kitchen table and carefully unwrapped it.

~

Jenny arrived at my place the next morning at 6:30. She threw her jacket on the sofa and took a seat. "Carl said he'd stop by and pick up Roxie this morning. Nicki's looking forward to having your cat stay at our house for the weekend."

"I'm glad that worked out. I'm curious how she'll react to your dog."

"Lucy will have a blast chasing Roxie everywhere."

I grimaced. "That's what I'm afraid of."

I showed Jenny the gift for Nicki and told her I'd opened the box and found a CD of Scotty Nelson, Nicki's favorite singer. "I re-wrapped the gift because I knew Nicki would like to open it."

Jenny tilted her head and narrowed her eyes. "You couldn't wait to find out what Wes gave Nicki, so you unwrapped it?"

I shook my head. "Suspicion, I guess. Why did he give a gift to my granddaughter when I'm engaged to Blake? I thought it was odd and wanted to check it out."

When the doorbell rang a few minutes later, Jenny and I greeted Blake and Allison and we made our way to Blake's car.

I zipped my jacket and gazed at the dark blanket of clouds overhead. *Reminds me of those dark days when I lived with my aunt. I hope it's not an indication of my visit with her.*

While we waited in line at airport security, Jenny, Allison, and Blake chatted.

What am I doing, Lord? What do I say to that woman? I still didn't feel any uncertainty about meeting Blake's mom, and his Aunt Debra, whose position I replaced at BCH, was a jewel. I was sure Mom would be too. But Aunt Mary?

When we neared our gate, seating was limited. We couldn't find four chairs together. We opted instead to sit across the concourse at an almost empty gate where we had a clear view of ours. Allison and Jenny took seats across from Blake and me. When he excused himself to take a walk, Allison scurried over and sat. "You'll never guess what I found online."

"A new mystery you're dying to read?"

She opened her eyes wide. "When I read, it must include romance." She fiddled with her cell and shoved it in front of my face. "This."

I gasped and placed my hand on my chest. "The dress you told me about last month? The one you saw in your dream?" I focused on a deep purple, lacey dress with a lavender lining. Allison dreamt of Blake and me getting married before she met me. The dress I wore in her dream was the one she showed me on her phone.

Allison beamed. She hugged me and bounced her feet up and down. "I'll order it, and have it shipped to you if you think this will work. If it's not the right size, we'll ship it back and try another."

I smiled at Jenny. "I think it will work, do you?"

She agreed. Allison closed the app on her phone when she saw Blake getting close. "Here comes Dad." She scooted back to her chair next to Jenny.

"What are you ladies up to?" Blake took his seat to the right of me.

"Wedding plans." I took his hand and squeezed. "Wish we knew a definite date."

"I left Andy a voicemail on Monday and Wednesday. If he'll talk with me, I may be able to smooth things over between us and address his concerns." Blake heaved a heavy sigh. "Let's ask the girls what they think." He directed his attention to Jenny and Allison. "Should we hold off and wait for Andy and Zoey to commit, or should we set a date and go with it?"

"If you go ahead, it will crush Zoey. Andy doesn't play fair." Allison sighed and slumped her shoulders. "I called him yesterday and chewed him out."

Blake leaned toward her. "How did he react?"

"Like the bumblehead he is."

I stood and motioned to Jenny and Allison to move closer to us. "Let's pray for Andy together."

Allison stared at me with her mouth opened. "Here? Now? In the airport?"

Blake rose. "We'll be quiet and discreet. They'll think we're having a confidential conversation." He smiled. "Keep your eyes open if it makes you feel better."

We brought our heads close together. I led a prayer for Andy and Zoey, and Jenny followed with one for me and my Aunt Mary's reunion.

Allison ended with, "And please don't let Grandmother scare Keedryn away. Amen."

I raised my eyebrows and peered at Blake.

He narrowed his eyes at Allison. "Go sit and hush." He wrapped his arm across my shoulder and pulled me close. "My mother will love you."

Twelve

Tampa, Florida

Blake rented an SUV, and we drove to The Cheesecake Factory near the airport for lunch. After our meal, we traveled south and west to a lovely, older two-story home on Old Tampa Bay. The fresh air and sunny skies lifted my anxiety until a petite, white-haired woman came into my view. She stood inside and peered out the front window. I took a deep breath and asked the Lord for strength.

Blake's Aunt Debra bolted out the front door. She hugged Allison, Jenny—whom she'd never met—and me before she embraced Blake. She stepped back from him. "You look like your old self." She turned to me again. "Thank you for your obedience to the Lord." She hurried into the house.

I stared at Blake. "What did she mean by that?"

He shrugged and shook his head. "I don't know." He held my hand and led me around back. "Mother will want us to visit on the lanai on a beautiful day like today."

After Mrs. Conner greeted Blake and Allison, she eyed me.

Blake said, "Mother—"

"This must be Keedryn." She narrowed her eyes at me and spoke in a haughty tone. "You're not whom I pictured." She glanced at Jenny. "But she's definitely your daughter." She grinned. "Let's sit while Debra prepares iced tea."

Blake pointed to the porch swing, but I didn't move. *Ask her in a kind way what she meant. Don't let your ire show.* "I'm sorry, Mrs. Conner, whom were you expecting?"

"Have a seat first." Blake's mom sat in a padded white, wicker chair along the screened windows.

Jenny and Allison shared a padded wicker bench positioned next to Mrs. Conner's chair.

Blake led me to the swing, and we sat across from the rest of the family with a beautiful view of the bay. "Mother, I'm curious too. I described her. Whom were you expecting?"

"I expected the type you brought home from college. Long-haired blondes in miniskirts who doted all over you." She looked me in the eye. "I hope this girl has brains."

Allison squirmed on the bench. "Grandmother, Mom wore her blonde hair long when she married Dad. Are you saying she didn't have brains?"

"No, of course not." She batted her hand in the air. "Your mother was the exception, although she doted on your father, she was the first girl that he brought home with common sense about her."

I relaxed in the swing, happy I'd kept my cool. No need to get peeved over hair color.

"Keedryn. Such an unusual name. I'd not heard it before Blake mentioned it. Was that a special family name?"

"My mother named me. But my aunt explained later why."

Mrs. Conner said, "Please tell us. I'm intrigued."

"When Mom found out she was pregnant, she felt lost. My dad took off, and my aunt encouraged her to abort me." I gazed out at the bay. "She met a lady who offered my mom a place to live until I was born. Because of this lady's kind heart and generous spirit, my mom named me after her." I glanced at Mrs. Conner.

She pulled down her glasses and looked at me over the rims. "Hmm. I suppose that's a tough name to wear. Kind and generous. I doubt your aunt agrees."

"Mother." Blake jumped to his feet. "Keedryn is my fiancée and your guest. How dare you treat her this way."

"Oh, shush. Who made you righteous and almighty? You told me yourself Keedryn hasn't seen her caregiver for thirty years."

Blake blocked my view of his mother.

I stood and stepped to his side to see Mrs. Conner. "I'll be happy to answer your question."

Blake turned to me and mouthed, "We can leave."

I shook my head, and Blake took his seat. "As I've already said, my aunt wanted me aborted. She never called me by my name. Instead, she badgered me, talked down to me, and when she addressed me, she called me K. She called me that because she didn't expect me ever to be kind or generous. She believed I'd be a terror." I returned to the swing.

Allison whispered something to Jenny and turned to Blake. "I'll check on Aunt Debra and ask if she needs help with the tea."

After Allison left the lanai, I continued. "When my

cousin, Vivian, who I often refer to as my sis, told me that Aunt Mary relocated to Florida near her, I asked if she needed any financial help. My late husband, Sam, and I sent a check each month, so Aunt Mary could afford a place to live and medical insurance. Vivian paid for her food, utilities, and provided transportation. We did this for eleven years." I peeked at Jenny, her eyes now wide.

I focused on Blake's mom. "We stopped our support when Sam became ill, and our bills mounted up. I've saved since he died to replenish our financial accounts. But when Aunt Mary moved in with Vivian, Viv said she could handle everything. Because I insisted, Viv never told my aunt about our support, so she'd say I am neither kind nor generous."

Jenny rose with tears in her eyes. "That's why Dad didn't buy me a newer car when I graduated from high school, isn't it? He said he couldn't afford it, which made little sense at the time but makes perfect sense considering what you just told us." She plodded toward the swing.

Blake and I scooted over to allow Jenny room to sit next to me. She laid her head on my shoulder. "I'm sorry I fought him on that."

I patted Jenny's leg. "He didn't expect you to understand then, but he'd be proud of you now."

Blake's mother stood tall with her shoulders back. "Keedryn. Take a walk with me. I'd like to show you my camellias." She led the way through the lanai and out the back door.

My heartrate soared. *Am I about to get chewed out or what?*

We strolled to the far side of the house where a

colorful shrub filled with pink flowers bloomed.

"Those are lovely, Mrs. Conner. I don't believe I've seen them before, and to have them grow in the winter must be a blessing."

She frowned. "My dear. Please call me Augusta. No more Mrs. Conner. And if you tell Blake what I'm about to say, I will deny it to my grave."

Her stern appearance put me in fight-or-flight mode. "I won't say a word."

"Welcome to our family." She smiled as though she won a grand prize. "You are an answer to our prayers." She picked a flower from the bush and handed it to me. "Any woman who can take my son from his former grumpiness and replace his forlorn expression with a look of love and admiration in his eyes, deserves my blessing. And to think he'd confront his mother over the woman he loves, I am proud to call you my daughter-in-law."

"Thank you, Augusta. That means a lot to me."

She hugged me and linked her elbow into mine while we ambled from the camellia shrub to the corner of her house. There, she lowered her arm. Funny woman. I guess she didn't want anyone on the lanai to see her touch me in such a fond way.

Blake held the back door open and grinned. "Did you enjoy the camellias?"

"Look." I lifted the flower. "They're beautiful."

He kissed my cheek. "Like you." He winked at his mother.

Debra and Allison served iced tea and cookies, and we chatted for the next few hours about life in Florida and the restaurant where we planned to dine for dinner. Fresh fish, lobster, crab, scallops, oysters, and shrimp.

What more could anyone ask? Except, I disliked seafood.

~

The smell of fish overpowered me when we walked into the restaurant. The hostess asked if we'd like to sit inside or out. Augusta and I spoke at the same time. But not with the same response. I needed the outdoors to endure the next hour or two. Was that a glare or did I observe a slight twinkle in her eye?

Augusta faced the hostess. "Outdoors will be fine." She led the way and Jenny followed.

Allison turned to me. "She must like you already. If that had been me, she would have told me I could go outdoors and eat alone, but she and the rest of the family would dine inside."

Blake agreed, and after Allison followed our leader, he whispered in my ear. "I saw Mother hug you when I glanced out the kitchen window. I knew you were special, but I never expected that to happen." Smiling, he placed his hand on my back and guided me through the doorway to our table.

Debra, Augusta, and Allison took their seats on one side, with Blake, me, and Jenny on the other. We all appreciated a stunning view of the water. I smelled fish, but with the light breeze it didn't bother me as much as it did when we were inside.

The waiter took Allison's order first and made his way around the table. I was next to last. Everyone ordered disgusting shrimp or crab legs. I straightened and pushed my shoulders back. "I'd like the grilled chicken sandwich, please, with a salad for my side."

All eyes grew wide, except for Jenny's. She exhaled, twisted her head to the left to speak into my ear. "Thank you." She glanced at the waiter. "I'll have a burger and fries." She smiled and handed him her menu.

Blake chuckled next to me.

Augusta leaned forward. "I may reconsider what I told you earlier." She sat back, crossed her arms, and smirked.

Allison looked at her grandmother. "What did you tell Keedryn earlier?"

"That's between us, dear." She directed another twinkle my way. "Have you selected a date yet? We must add it to our calendar."

"We're waiting on Andy and Zoey." I frowned.

Blake reached for my hand under the table. "He won't answer or return my calls. When I speak to him, we'll work this out."

Augusta shook her head. "From what you've told me over the phone, there's only one thing to do."

We all stared at her.

"Let me call him. He'll talk to me. I'll set him straight." She pulled out her cell phone. "Better yet, I'll Facetime him."

Andy answered right away. "Hello, Grandmother. How are you and Aunt Debra?"

"The only way we could be better is if you were here too." She paused. "I have visitors."

She turned the phone toward Allison, "Hi, Andy. We miss you."

Blake was next. "Hi, son. I'd love to talk with you soon."

Jenny and I together said, "Hi, Andy." I added, "Give Zoey my love." His eyes narrowed, but he nodded.

Debra was last. "Hello, dear. We'd love to have you visit us soon."

Augusta turned the phone back toward her. "I hate

to admit this out loud, but I love your father's selection in a new wife. We all know she can never take the place of your mother, but she's already blessed my heart. Whatever you have against her or your father must be forgiven. Do you understand?"

"I've got to go, Grandmother. I'll think about it."

"He hung up." She scowled and placed her phone faced down on the table. "I'll call him again from home."

I reached across the table for Augusta's hand, which rested on top of her phone. "Thank you."

She pulled her hand away. "Don't let it go to your head. I said what I needed to." The corners of her mouth curved upward.

Blake pulled out his cell and wrinkled his forehead. "I just received a text from Andy. He said he's praying about it." Blake looked up. "I didn't expect that from him. But thankful."

Our food arrived, and Augusta spread her palms and offered to pray. We all joined hands.

"Father, we thank you for this meal before us and for our family being together. We ask that You draw Andy closer to Your side. And may Your blessings be upon Keedryn tomorrow as she visits her aunt. Calm her heart and give her Your words to speak."

Thirteen

The following morning, Debra and Augusta whipped up a hearty breakfast of eggs, pancakes, bacon, and sausage. Blake helped with country potatoes, and I took on biscuits and gravy. Allison's fresh-squeezed orange juice was a hit, and Jenny set the table and provided everyone with whatever they needed.

"I won't need to eat for the rest of the day." Blake patted his stomach.

I stood and placed my hand on his shoulder. "You'll manage a bite before the day is over." I gathered my plate and Blake's and carried them to the sink.

After we cleaned the kitchen, we retreated to the lanai. Another beautiful day awaited us.

When Debra joined us, I asked, "What did you mean when you thanked me for my obedience to the Lord?"

She glanced at Allison. "Perhaps sweet Alli should answer your question, dear."

Allison's eyes darted around the lanai. She rose and stretched. "Time for my jog. Anyone care to join me?"

Blake wrinkled his forehead and spoke in a serious tone. "You can jog after you answer Keedryn's question."

Allison sighed and returned to her spot on the bench.

"A few of us got together several times to pray for Dad to find a new special someone. We wanted him to find healing for his broken heart and to fall in love again."

I leaned toward her. "Who's we?"

"When I first mentioned it to Aunt Debra, she agreed and suggested we include Beth Davis." She grinned. "Beth and Aunt Debra both said they knew the perfect person for Dad. You."

Debra's face beamed when she looked at me. "Dear, I knew you were the one for Blake. I felt in my heart that the two of you would fall in love, and I'm thankful you obeyed the Lord and pursued Blake with persistency."

"No." I jumped up. "I did no such thing."

Blake sat back on the swing and placed his hands behind his head with a smug look on his face. "Yes, you did." He patted the swing's cushion next to him.

I took my seat next to Blake again and wrinkled my nose at him.

"You wouldn't leave me alone, and you know it, sugarplum. Between your determination to win me over and the three ladies' prayers, the only thing left for me to do was to give in and fall in love with you." He pulled me close and dipped his head to kiss me on my cheek.

"That's not the way I remember it." I smacked him on his leg, and he laughed at me.

He whispered in my ear, "Will you go for a walk with me to the water's edge?"

"Sure. As long as you don't call me sugarplum again." I took his hand and we stepped out the back door and strolled to the water.

He nudged my shoulder. "What are your plans for today?"

"I called Vivian this morning before we prepared

breakfast. I left a voicemail, but she hasn't called back. Maybe they've gone on a cruise?" I lifted my eyes and smiled.

"You still don't want to visit your aunt, do you?"

"No. I don't. But I will since it means so much to you. Maybe we should drive by their house." I rubbed my palms on my pant legs. "Let's get this over with."

"Great." Blake took a step toward the lanai.

"No. Wait." I faced the water. "The butterflies in my stomach just turned into giant locusts."

He spun me to face him. "And God is surrounding you." Blake kissed the top of my head. "You can do this."

I nodded and made my way to the lanai, Blake by my side. I entered first and found Jenny on the porch swing. "We're ready to go. Are you?"

She jumped up. "Do you have the address with you? I have it if you don't."

Allison, Debra, and Augusta said they'd pray. I needed their prayers to get through this.

~

We drove east and then south to Gibsonton—a thirty-minute drive. Blake turned right off S. Tamiami Trail, made a left and drove to a dead end. We stopped outside a dilapidated bungalow which appeared smaller than my condo. Several shingles and cracked stucco needed repair, mildew covered the front door, and a weed paradise hid the yard.

I gaped at the house. "This isn't it. We're at the wrong place."

"But this is their street, and the address on the mailbox matches what you put into the GPS." Blake twisted and glanced at Jenny in the back seat. "Is this what you have?"

"This should be right."

"No. No. Vivian told me that she needed nothing. This can't be the place." Tears puddled in my eyes. "How could things have gotten this bad?"

The front door opened, and a woman who appeared to be in her mid-sixties zipped outside. Took me a moment to realize she was my cousin Vivian—a woman in her early fifties.

Jenny opened her car door and ran into Vivian's arms. Blake and I climbed out and waited for Vivian and Jenny to have their moment.

Viv clutched her chest and rushed toward me. "I should have answered your call. I was busy with Mom." She embraced me and her body shook. Her sobs broke my heart. "I can't believe you're here."

She pulled away, and I introduced her to Blake. "I'm happy to meet you." She took both of his hands in hers. "Thank you for coming." Vivian turned to me. "To have you here will thrill Mom."

"Thrill?"

"She's waited thirty years for you to come home."

Impossible. I blinked several times and looked at Blake and Jenny. "Thirty years?"

Vivian moved closer to me. "She told me a few years ago that to see you again has been her heart's desire for a long, long time. But she swore me to secrecy."

"Why?" I stared at my palms and took a step back.

Blake touched my elbow. "Are you okay?"

I peered at him and furrowed my eyebrows. "I'm not sure. None of this makes sense."

Vivian spoke just above a whisper. "Sis, she wanted you to come when you were ready to see her too. Not because I asked you to visit." Vivian led us to the front door. "She's napping but come on inside. I'll find her box."

"Box?"

"She has a few things for you that she's kept in a shoebox. I've never seen the contents, she keeps it sealed, but she'll want you to have it. She mentions it—and you—often." Viv told us to take a seat in the living room, and she slipped away. Blake and I sat in old, ratty chairs across from a shabby sofa. An old console TV sat in the front corner of the room.

What am I doing here? I chewed on my bottom lip and gripped the arms of my chair.

Blake reached over and rubbed my shoulders. "Breathe."

Jenny wandered around the room and gazed at photographs that hung on the walls. "Mom? Is this you?"

I rose and padded across frayed, avocado green carpet to Jenny, who studied pictures on the fireplace mantel. I picked up my senior graduation photo. "She displays this? Did she know we were coming for a visit?" I peered at Jenny.

"Why are you looking at me? I said nothing."

I returned to a chair next to Blake.

A few minutes later, Viv carried a taped-up shoebox into the living room and placed it under a chair next to the couch. I assumed that was Aunt Mary's chosen seat.

"Mom and I are so happy about your wedding."

I shook my head. "Aunt Mary is happy for me?" *No way.*

"Sis, she's changed. You'll see." Vivian straightened. "I hear her. I should tell her that you're here. She might die of a heart attack if she walks in and sees you." Viv stood and strolled down the hallway.

Blake reached over and took my hand. "Jenny and I are here for you. You're okay."

I listened to the voices down the hall.

"Who's here? Keedryn?" Aunt Mary's voice crackled as she spoke. "Vivian, I've told you before I'm too old for your nonsense. That girl will never forgive me for the way I treated her. Why would she come see me now? Am I dying? I don't have any money to give her."

I got up, then returned to my seat. To process what was about to happen boggled my mind. I rose again to run outside but stopped when Jenny and Blake both stood. I needed to face this woman who'd caused me much heartache. *Does she want to see me again? Why?*

My aunt came around the corner. I put my hand over my chest. She hobbled into the living room pushing a walker.

I stared at her, baffled by her frailty. If Vivian looked sixty-five, Aunt Mary could pass for ninety, but she was only seventy. Her eyes met mine. She pushed her walker closer to me and raised her shaky hand. "God has answered my prayers. Child, I'm sorry for the grief I caused you—"

My mind went numb. *Did she say she's sorry?*

Vivian took her by the elbow. "Mom, you need to sit." She turned Aunt Mary around and directed her to the chair.

"Leave me be. I'm not done with Keedryn."

"She can move her chair closer to you. You must sit."

She called me Keedryn. She hated my name. But she's said it twice and said it with kindness both times.

And she's prayed for me to visit her? My heart softened.

Blake picked up my chair and moved it closer to my aunt.

In a rougher tone, my aunt said, "Who are these other people? What are they doing here with you?"

Now, that sounded like Aunt Mary. I pointed to Jenny on the couch. "My daughter, Jenny."

Jenny rose and walked toward Aunt Mary. "Hi. I'm happy to meet you."

"Come closer. My eyesight's not all that great."

Jenny knelt in front of my aunt's chair.

"You're a pretty thing like your mother." She smiled.

Aunt Mary smiled at my baby girl. That broke another hole in the wall that surrounded my heart.

"And him? Who let him inside?"

"He's my fiancé, Blake. We're getting married soon."

Vivian patted Aunt Mary's shoulder. "Remember, I told you about their wedding."

I reached for Blake's hand. "My first husband, Jenny's dad, died a few years ago. The Lord has blessed me with another man who loves me."

Aunt Mary's walker was still between us. She pulled herself up to her five-foot height, lifted one hand, and pointed her bony finger in Blake's face. "You treat her well or you'll answer to me young man. She's endured enough heartache with me as her guardian. Never again will I allow anyone to treat her poorly."

"Aunt Mary, I plan to cherish her forever." He and Jenny returned to their seats.

My aunt sat and clasped her hands together. "Vivian said she put a box under my chair. Where is it?"

Vivian moved Aunt Mary's walker out of the way, and I reached underneath and pulled out the shoebox.

"Thank you, hon." She placed it next to her. "First, can you forgive me? I was hateful. Cruel. Won't make excuses. Just plain ornery."

I took her fingers in my hands and focused on her eyes. "Aunt Mary, I forgave you many years ago. I've struggled since with resentment, but the Lord reminds me of what Christ did on the cross for me and how He suffered."

"People treated Him bad too, didn't they?"

"Yes. And He forgave them. And I forgive you now for everything that happened. I love you with God's love, and hope you can forgive me, too, for any trouble I caused you."

Tears streamed down her face. "There's nothing to forgive you for, my child." She looked around until she spotted Viv, who stood behind her. "Where's my Bible?"

Viv stepped away, returned a minute later with a Bible, and handed it to her mother.

Aunt Mary said, "I want you girls to help me understand. I've been filled with doubt and find it hard to believe Keedryn could forgive me, but here she is. I want to believe God will forgive me too."

Aunt Mary lifted the Bible from her lap with both hands and gave it to me.

I flipped through the pages to 1 John 1:9. Aloud, I read, "If we confess our sins, he is faithful and just and will forgive us our sins and purify us from all unrighteousness." I reached for my aunt's hands again. "We confess, and He forgives."

I glanced over my shoulder at Blake and mouthed, "Pray." He rose, came closer, and led us in prayer. Aunt

Mary repeated many of the words after him. When we finished, I hugged her neck.

Vivian handed us both tissues and the shoebox that had fallen on the floor.

Aunt Mary tugged at the tape that surrounded the box but struggled. Blake pulled out his pocketknife and offered to help. He cut the tape around the box and handed it back to my aunt before he returned to his seat.

Aunt Mary's hands shook when she pulled off the top. She laid the lid next to her and stared inside. "Keedryn, honey, I should have given this to you before you left for college, but I didn't think fast enough. I planned to share this with you on your eighteenth birthday. I'm sorry I didn't get it to you."

"You couldn't send it if you didn't know where I lived." I covered her trembling hands with mine. "Please don't blame yourself."

"I blame myself for a lot of things. I hope today I can make it right." She pulled out a handful of old photos and gave them to me.

The first was of Dad and Mama on their wedding day. Next, a photo of Dad while he talked or sang to me when I was a baby. The third one was of Mama and me while we played dress up when I was five. She had allowed me to help her with her makeup. Her face was a mess.

Tears welled when I looked at a picture of my parents and me on my tenth birthday, a few days before they died. Aunt Mary took the photo before I blew out my candles.

I hope that box is almost empty. I can't take much more of this.

Aunt Mary pulled something out of the box. I

covered my mouth. *Oh, God, help me. Mama's pearls.* I couldn't move.

Aunt Mary's hand shook as she held them out to me.

I opened my palm and she gently placed them there. "She wore these the night she died." I turned to Blake. "The ones I told you about."

He stood, strode closer to me, and laid his hand on my shoulder. "They're beautiful." He kissed my cheek. "Do you need a break before you see anything else?"

Aunt Mary peered at Blake. "There are only more photos, and she can look at those later."

"If Aunt Mary doesn't mind, I need fresh air." I rose, took a step, and everything went dark.

Fourteen

I rested against our rental car. Blake stood on one side of me and Jenny on the other. Both fussing over me. "I'm fine. To see those photos overwhelmed me. And Mama's pearls? I'm sorry, that tore me up."

Jenny rubbed my shoulder. "You have every reason to be emotional. You expected Aunt Mary to be mean and hateful, but she welcomed you as she would royalty. She lavished you with sentimental gifts and asked you and the Lord for forgiveness. That's a lot to take in, all in less than an hour."

Blake faced me and placed both hands on my upper arms. "I'm proud of you. You didn't know what to expect from your aunt, but you handled yourself in a gracious manner." He held me close and told me again how much he loved me.

I pulled away, eyed the overgrown grass and weeds, and made my way to the front door. "They need my help."

Blake and Jenny agreed.

We entered the house and Aunt Mary grinned. "Are you feeling better, Keedryn?"

I nodded and thanked her for her concern. I sat in the chair positioned in front of hers and took a deep breath.

"While you enjoyed the fresh air, I asked Vivian to fetch me this old Bible. I found it in your parent's possessions. Belonged to your daddy. I'm sure he'd want you to have it."

I took it from her outstretched arms and flipped open the cover where I read an inscription. "Looks like he received it when he was a teenager." I brought it to my chest. "I'll cherish it."

She touched her temple and closed her eyes. "I was angry with God for taking them from you and taking your mom from me. That's when I took to drinking." Her voice choked with tears. "When you came to live with me, and you mentioned Jesus, I became angrier. I've already told you how sorry I am for all that." She scanned the room. "I'm feeling a little light-headed, hon."

I leaned back in my chair and looked over my shoulder at Blake. "Aunt Mary seems exhausted, and I am too. We should go so she can rest."

Blake looked at Aunt Mary. "Is there anything you need before we leave tomorrow?"

"No, hon. We're doing fine." She glanced at Vivian. "Aren't we?"

She agreed.

When we stood to leave and said our goodbyes, I pulled Viv aside and spoke to her about support money.

Not sure how long Aunt Mary would be with us, and I wanted to give her the best care possible. *I wish I'd visited her sooner. I wasted so many years.*

~

Blake pulled the rental into a fast-food restaurant's drive-through lane along Tamiami Trail. Three cars waited in front of us. "We're on our own for a few hours. We'll pick up lunch, and after we eat, I have a treat for you both if K's not too tired."

Jenny smacked her hands together. "Does that mean a trip to the beach?"

Blake twisted in his seat and stared at Jenny with his mouth opened. "Do you think the only reason to come to Florida is for the beach?"

"No, of course not. Either that or Disney World, but because we're closer to the beach, I hope that's where you'll take us."

He gazed at me. "What would you like to do for a few hours? Return to Mother's for a nap, the beach, or see alligators?"

Jenny squealed and clapped several times. "Gators sounds like fun. Let's do it."

I turned to Jenny and frowned. "Must you squeal in my ear and make so much noise? You act like your daughter." I shook my head and eyed Blake. "What did you hope to do?"

"We're close to Myakka River State Park. We should be able to spot a few alligators there. Tonight, we can view the sunset from Clearwater Beach if you'd like. We can invite Mom and Aunt Debra to join us."

Jenny gripped the back of my headrest. "Yes. We get to do both. Carl will be jealous when he finds out I saw gators *and* the beach."

Jenny acted like she'd never been to Florida. I knew that wasn't true. We'd seen alligators on our last family trip there, although that had been ten years earlier.

I rolled my eyes and peered at Blake. "Some kids never grow up."

We placed our order, picked it up at the window, and drove to a nearby park. Jenny hurried to one of the three picnic tables close to a live oak draped in Spanish moss.

We discussed how much Aunt Mary had changed and how ill she appeared after years of alcohol abuse and other health issues. I mentioned my concern that she may not live long.

Jenny straightened and cleared her throat. "I'd like to help, too, toward Aunt Mary's care. I'm sure Carl will agree. How can we do that without her or Aunt Viv getting upset with us?"

"When I hugged Viv goodbye, I told her I'd send money again. She balked, but I insisted. I'll take care of it, Jenny. You don't need to do anything."

She spoke with compassion. "But I want to. They're my family too. The only other relative I have is Uncle Bud on Dad's side, and he doesn't need any help."

I reached across the picnic table and rested my hand on top of hers. "Okay. When we get home, let's figure out together what we can give to help them out on a regular basis."

Blake's face softened. "Their immediate need is different housing. And a better car. I'll help with those."

Jenny chuckled. "Yeah. That old clunker won't last much longer."

He stood and gathered our trash. "One of you may want to check to see if they have any medical bills that need paid."

"That's sweet, Blake, but we should wait until after the wedding for you to help. I'll call Viv next week and ask her about medical bills. We can search places to live on the Internet and make suggestions to her after we're married."

"Buttercup, their need is urgent. I can help before the wedding. Where do you come up with these rules?" He scrunched his face and threw our trash into the garbage can.

"The journal of etiquette." I chuckled. "Apparently, you haven't read it."

Jenny giggled.

Blake shook his head. "What does Vivian do for a living?"

I explained that Viv currently worked at cleaning houses and businesses to allow her flexible hours to look after Aunt Mary.

I rose and grabbed my water cup. "And where did you find these pet names? A list on Google?"

Blake frowned. "Yes. I jotted down a few and check my list from time to time." He glared at me. "If you don't like these, help me come up with something you like."

"The best name will be one you create all on your own that says something about me. Take into consideration my personality or what you admire in me." I winked at Jenny.

"I admire buttercups." He grinned. "They're a beautiful yellow flower, and their petals shine."

"Sweet. Do you think I'm beautiful and sparkly?"

He hesitated, which told me that he picked a name off his list and not because he thought I fit the description.

"Sure?"

This time I glared at him.

"Yes, that's why I chose buttercup." He opened his eyes wide.

I shook my head and raised my eyebrows.

Jenny stood and took a sip of her lemonade. "I'm ready for alligators. How long will it take us to get there?"

"The park's an hour south of us." Blake threw the

rest of his drink away and held my elbow. "Are you up to this, or would you rather relax and process all that happened with your aunt?"

I glanced at Jenny.

"Mom, you know I'd give up the gators for you."

"Let's get going." I patted Jenny's arm. "I'm ready to spend a few hours with two of my favorite people at the park."

We spent a couple of hours there and saw plenty of waterfowl, alligators, turtles, and lizards. I loved the gracefulness of the herons, and Jenny's favorites, of course, were the gators.

Blake wrapped his right arm across my shoulder and his left around Jenny's. "My favorite part was watching the enjoyment on your faces, but we need to get back to Tampa and Clearwater Beach so K and I can enjoy a romantic sunset."

Fifteen

Allison greeted us in the front yard of Augusta's home and told us her grandmother and aunt were exhausted after a full afternoon of activities. I thought we should stay and visit and forget the beach, but Jenny protested.

Blake turned toward her. "We can leave your mom here, and I'll take you young ladies to the beach. I'm ready for sand between my toes."

I slapped Blake's arm. "If you plan a trip to the beach, I want to come along. But won't your mother feel deserted?"

"Let's see what she wants. She may prefer the quiet with all of us gone."

When we checked in with Augusta, she insisted we go on without them.

We drove west for thirty-five minutes and chatted about the lovely weather and the magnificent homes on the bay. The conversation turned serious when Allison asked Blake if he'd heard anything new regarding the police investigation about Eliza's death.

He shook his head. "Nothing at all. I hope that means we're no longer suspects."

We all nodded. *That will be one less thing to stress*

over while planning a wedding.

We arrived at Clearwater Beach just before sunset and enjoyed the beautiful white sand. Bright yellow and deep orange lit the sky while the sun set. Blake and I waded along the shore to the north where pink swirls gathered in the wispy clouds, while Jenny and Allison wandered to the south. They said they wanted us to delight in the romantic setting without them along.

"Our daughters are thoughtful." Blake took my hand and squeezed.

I stopped and gazed into his eyes. "Yes, they are."

He smiled and pushed a strand of hair behind my ear. "You're staring at me like you want something. A kiss, perhaps?"

"That would be amazing."

He kissed my lips and held me close. "There's something special about a kiss on the beach with the woman I love."

"I hope we have the opportunity to do this often."

We walked hand in hand and turned back to find the girls for dinner.

Blake released my hand and pulled out his cell. "My gardener. Excuse me." He brought the phone to his ear. "Hello . . . What?" He stopped walking and listened. "How much damage? . . . I don't believe this. Did you call the police? . . . Do it now. I'll call Jim and see if he can come over and help you out . . . Thanks for calling."

"What happened?"

"In a minute. I need to call Jim first." Blake's face turned red, and his left fist clenched. "Hey. Can you go over to my house and check in with Hank? He's around back at the greenhouse. Someone trashed the place . . . I told him to call the police. Make sure they get a report and include anything stolen . . . We'll be home tomorrow around 3:00 p.m."

I grabbed Blake's arm with both hands. "Someone vandalized your greenhouse?"

He spoke in a stern tone. "Who do you think would do such a thing, K? Huh?"

"Blake, why would Wes do this? And how did he know you had a greenhouse to vandalize?"

"He may have looked out the back window during our engagement party."

I lifted my hands and jogged fifty feet toward Jenny and Allison. "I give up."

"What's wrong, Mom?" Jenny touched my arm.

"That man. He's impossible."

Jenny looked at Allison. "I guess their walk wasn't all that romantic."

Blake joined us and explained what happened with the greenhouse and shared his thoughts about Wes being the likely suspect.

Jenny turned to me. "Mom, perhaps you should consider Wes as a strong possibility."

Blake shook his head. "Maybe you can convince her. I haven't had much success. She won't accept that this—"

"But if he knew there was a greenhouse, he didn't know Blake sent me roses." I placed my hands on my hips. "I never discussed them with him."

Allison raised her eyebrows. "Tauni knew. She's someone else who could be responsible."

I plodded toward the parking lot where we left the car. *Wes acted strange Thursday, but he wouldn't do this. And no way could Tauni be involved.*

Blake took hold of my arm. The girls stood behind

him. "Let's get dinner. The four of us will talk this through and try to figure out whom—Tauni or Wes— might be responsible. Okay?"

I yanked my arm away and kept walking.

~

We sat in a booth in a pizza place we found near the beach. I wanted to sit with Jenny, but I'd have to look at Blake. Easier to sit next to him, but he wanted to hold my hand, and I let him. No use making a scene. We placed our order and Jenny asked the hostess for a piece of paper and a pencil.

I scrunched my face. "What's that for?"

"We can keep a list of why we consider it's one of them or the other." Jenny grinned.

"Here we go again." I frowned and shook my head. "You and your lists."

When Jenny was ready, Blake rubbed his hand down his face. "Can't be Tauni. She got a promotion. That wouldn't make any sense at all."

After a lengthy sigh, I said, "Not Tauni or Wes." *Blake wears me out.* "Could there be someone we haven't considered yet?"

"Right." Blake's words leaked sarcasm. "Like whom?"

I glared at him. "Think a minute. Who else could have it out for you? I don't imagine it's only Wes."

He flinched and crossed his arms. "What are you saying exactly? You assume that I have a lot of enemies?"

Jenny straightened. "What about your former HR director—Miranda, right? She lost her job because of you. Or the VP of Legal? He'd be mad at you too."

Allison's eyes grew wide and she gasped. "There's

also Eliza's daughter, Cindy." Her eyes darted between Blake and me. "If she believes her mother was murdered, she could presume Dad had something to do with it."

A smug smile crossed my lips. "Those are potential possibilities. Blake?"

He shook his head. "None of those people were guests at our party. Someone tried to implicate Andy, remember?"

"But what if that was a fluke? An innocent comment like I mentioned earlier. Let's look at the last two crimes and forget the party guests for a minute."

Blake rested his elbow on the table and placed his palm on his forehead. "So, either Miranda, Lance, or Cindy parked in BCH's parking lot and waited for my arrival so after all the employees arrived, they could key my car. Then they showed up at my house today to destroy my greenhouse."

The three of us ladies at the table looked at one another and nodded together. Allison said, "Sounds possible."

He glanced around at us. "I can see one of them vandalizing my car. But why the greenhouse and not my house windows?" He glared at me. "The greenhouse is the clue here. Is there any chance Wes knew about the roses?"

Jenny held her pencil over the paper. "Did you receive any roses at the office Wes might have seen?"

"No."

"How many times has Wes been at your condo?" She gazed at me, her eyes bright.

"On Thanksgiving before Blake arrived." I peered at Blake. "But you brought in a bouquet of roses after Wes pulled out of the parking lot."

Blake laid his arm across my shoulder. "And a few days before Christmas when I saw you and Wes at the Gaylord Opryland Hotel."

"He didn't pick us up. He met Nicki and me there."

Jenny scribbled a note. "What about the night before? I dropped Nicki off, and Wes came by and took you both to see Christmas lights."

"That's right." I paused, squinted, and slowed my speech. "He came inside for a few minutes. I needed to get our coats from the hall closet."

Allison said, "Were there any roses in sight?"

I tilted my head. "I don't remember any."

Jenny's eyes lit. "I do. A salmon colored rose was in a bud vase on your coffee table. I noticed it when I dropped Nicki off."

"Okay. But he didn't know who it came from, or if he figured it out, I doubt he'd connect it to the greenhouse."

Jenny tapped her pencil up and down on her paper. "Maybe not, but Nicki knew. I told her about Papa Blake's greenhouse and the salmon-colored roses."

The waitress interrupted our conversation to apologize for the delay on our pizza. She explained a large to go order came in just before we placed ours.

After she stepped away, Blake moved his arm off my shoulder and folded his hands on the table. "Do you think Nicki would remember whether she or Wes talked about the rose if we call her?"

I arched my brow at Jenny. "She remembers everything that has to do with her papa."

Jenny pulled out her phone and clicked on Carl's number. She put the phone on speaker so we could all listen. "Hi, Mommy. I miss you."

"Hi sweetie. Nana and Papa are both with me."

After Nicki spoke to us, Jenny asked, "Did Mr. Wes ask about the rose on Nana's table the night he drove you to look at Christmas lights?"

I held my breath. *Please say no.*

"Yep. I told him it was from my papa, and he grew it all by himself."

I closed my eyes, and Jenny finished her call. *Blake can't be right.*

Blake took my hand in his. I guess he felt I needed comforting.

"Wait," I said. "Cindy, Miranda, or Lance may not be aware of the roses, but if they came onto your property to vandalize something, they'd know your house was alarmed. They chose the greenhouse because they didn't expect that to trigger anything."

Blake leaned back in the booth. "There's still the matter of my messed-up PowerPoint presentation at the healthcare conference in November."

"What? We determined that was Miranda two months ago."

He shook his head. "Nope. She admitted that she asked Lance to watch your condo and follow you, instructed him to take pictures of us together, and that they started the rumors. When Chad questioned her about my slides, she laughed and said that was too petty for her. She said someone else must have done it— probably Tauni. But it could have been Wes."

Our pizzas arrived and were devoured by three hungry people. I couldn't eat.

Sixteen

Mid-January
Nashville, Tennessee

Soon after I arrived at the office on Monday morning and while I typed at my computer, Blake stopped by to see me. "Good morning, sugar. Were you able to relax after I dropped you off yesterday?"

I shrugged. "Do we have plans tonight? I'd like to stay home and chill."

He pushed the adjoining door to Jocelyn's office closed and rested against it. "Is that your way to tell me that you don't want to get together this evening?"

"I'm stressed over this rift between us." I picked up my stapler, stared at it, and pushed it up and down while I spoke in a grumpy tone. "Would be better if I spent more time alone and pray."

Blake took the stapler from my hand. "Do I need to cancel the meeting with my attorney again? I rescheduled it for this afternoon at 4:30."

I glanced at him. "My will is at home. I'll pick it up at lunch. This afternoon will be fine."

He returned the stapler to my desk. "K, I know I've

been a little pushy over this thing with," he lowered his voice, "Wes. I realize how difficult this is for you. I'll drop it until we have proof." He observed the mess I'd made on my desk and frowned. "And I can see where Miranda, Lance, or Cindy could have a beef with me."

"Thank you." I scraped the wasted staples together, brushed them into my hand, and peeked into the hallway. "Have you seen Tauni this morning?"

"She stopped by to see me. She asked if she could train Terri this morning and planned to join me after morning break."

I gaped at Blake and threw the staples into the trash container under my desk. "You've become a softie too. You would have demanded I be there to assist you in case you needed something." I wrinkled my nose. "Like a paper clip."

He chuckled. "I don't believe I was that bad, sweet pea."

I shook my head. "Neither sugar nor sweet pea."

He left my office with a grin on his face.

~

Robin, the admin assistant from IT, arrived for her scheduled appointment at 8:30 a.m. I stood, closed my outer door, and offered her a chair.

She spoke with a shaky voice. "My problem is with Wes. I understand he's a friend of yours, so I wanted to talk with you before I said anything to my manager or Jocelyn."

I tilted my head and sat at my desk. "What seems to be the issue?"

"The past two weeks he's changed. A lot. He's been needy, pushy, and a pain."

"Can you give me examples?" I opened our HR

database to pull up his record and make notes of her concerns.

"He keeps coming to me for things. Supplies he can find in our cabinets or downstairs in the supply room. Paper clips, notepads, pens." She shifted in her chair. "Did he ask you for stuff when you were an assistant in IT?"

"Not that I remember." I typed in her remarks. "What else?"

"One minute he pesters me about something and the next he flirts and asks me to lunch or a movie." She narrowed her eyes. "If I tell my 250-pound, six-foot, six-inch, boyfriend about this, Wes won't live beyond tomorrow." She narrowed her eyes and frowned.

"I understand, but I hope you'll wait to tell your boyfriend until we can investigate this situation."

"I've told Wes no to his date offers several times, but he won't give up." Robin raised her voice and shook her head. "I can't get my work done when he bothers me all the time."

After finishing my notes, I told Robin I'd talk with Jocelyn and one of us would contact her soon. I needed to carefully phrase my next question. I didn't want to put words in her mouth. "In as few words as possible, how would you describe his overall actions toward you?"

She glanced around my office. "I've already told you. He's pushy, needy, and a pain." Her eyes focused on a book on my shelf. "Harassment. That describes his recent actions toward me."

"Are you aware of anyone who's witnessed Wes's behavior toward you?"

"He's too smart for that. I doubt anyone else knows about this."

"Not a problem. We'll handle this as discreetly as we can and talk with your manager too. He needs to be informed of what's happening in his department. You may need to sign a formal complaint. Are you willing to do that?"

She nodded and stood. "Thanks."

I smiled. "You did the right thing to come to me."

A few minutes after she left, Jocelyn entered my office through our connecting doors. "I saw Robin leave your office." She sat across from me. "Is everything okay in IT?"

"No." I twisted my monitor toward her. "She voiced a complaint against Wes. All here in his record."

Jocelyn shook her head. "My guess is this has something to do with you and Blake. He seems to have difficulty letting you go."

"He never had me. We were only friends. Anything else is a figment of his imagination."

"The problems go beyond Robin."

I leaned toward her. "What do you mean?"

"Kent has encountered a few issues with Wes too."

"Kent Jeffreys, our IT manager?"

"He came in to see me on Friday and told me Wes's work quality and attitude have declined since the holidays. Kent and I have a meeting scheduled with him tomorrow morning at 9:30. I'd like you to attend and share what Robin told you."

"Do I have to? All the notes are here in the database. You don't need me."

"I'll mention the new policy to him, but because you talked with Robin, you should be the one to represent her in the meeting." Jocelyn rose. "Part of the job." She returned to her office.

What does this mean? All along I believed Wes couldn't be involved in the vandalism because it's not who he is. But what Robin and Jocelyn told me isn't him either. *Lord, has Blake been right all along?* I needed to tell Blake about Kent's and Robin's concerns.

I poked my head inside Jocelyn's door. "May I share all of this recent information about Wes with Blake?"

"As the executive vice president, he'll be pulled into it anyway, so it's no problem. He has access to Wes's employee record. I finished updating my notes."

I returned to my desk and completed several outstanding tasks.

Blake popped his head in just before noon. "Join me for lunch? We can run by your place first and pick up your will for this afternoon's meeting."

Even with the friction between us over family matters and vandalism, he wanted to spend time with me. But I craved solitude.

"I've endured a crazy morning. Could I take a raincheck? I'd like to go home and relax with my feet propped for a few minutes." I stood and touched his arm. "Is that okay?"

"No problem."

"But I've changed my mind about dinner. I'll join you after our appointment with the attorney if your offer still stands."

"Sounds good. I thought you'd be interested to know I talked with Andy. But I suppose it can wait until tonight since you don't want to have lunch with me." He sulked and walked out my door.

"Blake, wait."

He shrugged and made his way down the hall.

I hope he tells me about Andy before I tell him about

Wes, because I have a feeling we'll end up in a fight over this too.

~

My afternoon flew by despite my weariness over the following day's meeting with Wes. Would Blake want to attend? I gathered my purse and jacket, said goodnight to Jocelyn, and hurried to Blake's office.

Tauni greeted me. "I've experienced the best first day. Ever."

"What made today special?"

"Blake." She stared toward his open door.

I glanced at Blake, who'd stepped out of his office and raised my eyebrows. "Wow. What did you do to earn such high praise?"

"I welcomed her with a gift or two. I'm trying to earn back the coveted 'boss of the year award.'"

Tauni chuckled. "He's got my vote. After lunch, he brought me a Starbucks latte and a gift card."

I looked at Tauni. "Did you say someone who gives gifts makes an excellent boss?"

"Not necessarily. They also must be friendly, flexible, and build up their staff by giving them the tools they need for success. Oh, and treat everyone as equals and allow them to work independently."

Blake grinned. "That's me. Ask Keedryn."

I wrapped my arm around his elbow and steered him toward the door. "Yes, dear."

We caught the elevator down and headed out to the parking lot.

Blake took my hand. "I think it's best, cupcake, if we both drive to the attorney's office."

I shook my head. "No cupcakes or cookies. I'll get fat hearing you use my new name." I gazed at him. "Why two cars? Is his office closer to where we live?"

"Yes. When we leave there, we'll run your car home and take mine to dinner."

We climbed into our vehicles and drove to Matt Starnes' office.

~

Mr. Starnes' assistant welcomed us, notified him of our arrival, and escorted us to his door. A balding man of medium build and around my age rose and greeted us. He shook Blake's hand and introduced himself to me with his hand extended. He seemed nice enough.

We took our seats, and he said to me, "I'm pleased to meet the woman who captured this guy's heart." He pointed to Blake. "We've known each other for many years, and he only recently became his old self again. You are an answer to many prayers."

I looked at Blake and smiled. To Matt, I said, "Sweet. Thank you." I liked this man.

He took a folder from the cabinet behind him and placed it on his desk. "Did you bring your will?"

I pulled an envelope out of my purse and held it in front of me.

"Great. Let's review this other form first, then we can look at your will. Blake's already given me his information, and once we add yours, you can sit down together and go over everything."

He took a form from his file folder and passed it over to me.

My heart raced and my stomach ached. I scanned in disbelief the first page of the document before me. I jumped up and glared at Blake. "Are you for real? We couldn't talk about this in private first? You brought me in here without warning and shoved this in my face?"

He stood and opened his eyes wide. "K. This is an important document. Protects both of us."

I shook my head. "This is low. I can't believe you care about me at all." I stormed out of Mr. Starnes' office and took off down the hallway as fast as I could go. *A prenuptial agreement? How could he? And why would he?*

Blake came from behind me, grasped my arm, and stopped me before I got to the outer door. He spoke in a calm tone. "We need this agreement. Prenups are for couples who've accumulated assets and must be wise in managing them. This affects us both."

"Expecting us to get a divorce before we've married doesn't sound like building our marriage on a solid foundation to me. Does it to you?" I grimaced.

"Not just about divorce. Covers circumstances related to death too."

I stared at the floor and gritted my teeth. "If you're finished bothering me, I'd like you to take your hand off my arm. I want to go home." I jerked my arm from his hold and rushed to my car.

Blake followed. After I opened my car door, he tossed a folder inside, and it landed on my seat. "Look at what I've already added to the form." He sounded irritated. "Call me and we'll discuss." He turned away, stepped toward the door of the building, and swung back around. "Forgive me for bothering you. Won't happen again." He continued into Matt's office building.

I picked up the folder and tossed it to the passenger side floor.

Seventeen

Tuesday morning came too soon. Why had I accepted the HR position knowing I'd see Blake? I'd see him today, and that made me angry. He made me angry. I shook my head. Hopefully, I could avoid him.

I came up with a brilliant idea and opened Jocelyn's adjoining door. "I'd like to work in one of the meeting rooms downstairs today."

She raised her eyebrows.

"I need a change of scenery to be more productive."

"Blake problems?"

I stared at the floor and shuffled my feet. "You could say that." I sighed. "I shouldn't have taken this position. He and I seem to disagree on everything, and we bring it to the office. I'm not a talented actress and can't hide my frustration well. I guess you should post my job. Maybe I can stay until you hire someone to take my place."

"I'm sure you're overreacting." She glanced at her computer screen. "Take a week to think this through, discuss it with Blake, and get back with me on Monday. Then we'll talk."

"You don't understand. I don't want to talk to him about anything right now."

She peeked behind me to the hallway. "Too bad because he's striding down the hall toward my office."

"I'll slip into my—"

"Good morning, ladies." He smiled. "I hope I'm not interrupting anything." He stood to my left, about an arm's length away.

"I was just leaving." I entered my office and closed the adjoining door. *Seems like he handles the role of actor well.*

I rushed down the hallway to visit Beth. After we chatted for a minute, I told her I planned to look for another job.

"But I seldom see you now and you're just down the hall. I'll never get to see you if you leave BCH." She rose and pointed to the conference room. "Would you like to talk about it?"

Inside, I told her about my latest struggles with Blake and how he wanted a prenup agreement and he'd already completed part of the form without me.

"Why did that upset you? A common practice these days. My brother's a lawyer and recommends it to his clients who are getting married, most often to couples over thirty."

"But aren't they written so when there's a divorce, they'll know what happens to their assets? A license to walk away and not try to work things out if you ask me."

"What did he already add to the form? Did you sense he wasn't being fair?"

"I haven't reviewed it."

"Perhaps you should start there." She stood. "If you haven't set a date yet, it might be wise to extend it out several months. I'm not sure you're ready to marry so soon." Beth walked back into her office, and I plodded down the hall to mine. *Not ready? I am ready. But Blake needs to change.*

When I sat, a reminder appeared on my calendar. Meeting regarding Wes Thomas to begin in fifteen minutes. I took a deep breath, closed my eyes, and prayed.

A quiet knock on my door caused me to look up. Blake.

"Sorry if I'm bothering you, but I wanted to inform you that I won't be able to attend your meeting with Wes today. Jocelyn told me about it."

I sighed. "You're not bothering me."

"Well, since your meeting takes place in a few minutes, I'll leave you alone. Jocelyn said you can fill me in afterward." He turned and headed toward his office.

We were meeting Wes in the conference room in five minutes. I grabbed my notes and a pen and hurried back down the hall. Jocelyn and Kent sat across from one another at the table. I took a seat next to Jocelyn.

Wes arrived and sat next to Kent. "What's this all about?"

Jocelyn did her best to put Wes at ease. When she asked if he was aware of BCH's harassment policy, he jerked his head back and opened his eyes wide.

He peered at me. "Have I done anything to cause you to think I harassed you?"

Jocelyn shook her head. "No, Wes. This isn't about Keedryn." She glanced at me. "Tell Wes about your visitor yesterday."

Without mentioning her name, I told him a female employee accused him of harassment and why she felt that way.

He gaped at me and cocked his head. "Are you sure? She must have read me all wrong. I didn't mean to upset Robin. I was being friendly."

Kent pointed his pen at Wes. "Best thing you can do is to leave her alone. No more friendliness."

Wes grimaced and hunched his shoulders. "Um, okay."

"I'll monitor this situation and check in with her often, as will Keedryn and Jocelyn. I suggest that you talk to her only when necessary."

Wes looked down and rubbed his fingers across his forehead. He sounded flustered. "Of course."

Jocelyn's tone hardened. "Are you aware of our new policy on dating which stipulates employees cannot date someone from the same department?"

Wes nodded.

"Kent, share with Wes your observations," Jocelyn sat back in her chair.

Kent cleared his throat. "You've been a stellar employee since I took over as your manager five years ago. However, these past couple of weeks something's changed. I'm not sure of the reason, but team members came to me last week and complained about your attitude."

"What?" Wes stiffened.

"And I've observed your work quality has dropped. Is there anything I can do to help bring back the excellent employee who's given much to our department and company over the years?"

Wes stared at the table. "I'll work on these things. Unless you plan to fire me."

Jocelyn tapped her pen on her notepad and informed Wes this would go on his record as a warning. If there were further concerns, another meeting would be scheduled, and probation would result. She leaned forward. "We offer an employee assistance program that may help you if you're interested."

Wes stood and thanked us. He and I stepped into the hallway where he asked, "Do you have a few minutes? I'd like to talk with you about something."

~

Wes followed me to my office and took a seat. I kept the door open to the hallway.

He looked around before he focused on me. "I didn't mean to harass her. I'd like to apologize. Is that permissible?"

"I'm new at this. Let me see if Jocelyn is back in her office." I rose and walked to her door and peeked inside. "Not yet. I'll ask her later and get back with you." I wanted Wes to leave, but he remained seated, so I returned to my chair.

Wes fidgeted. "There's something I must confess to you. To you and Blake."

Oh no. Not the vandalism. "Go ahead." My chest felt heavy.

"When I heard you planned to travel to New Mexico with Blake for the conference you attended last November, jealousy consumed me. I messed with his presentation slides in hopes to make him look bad."

I stared at him with my mouth opened.

"Since my record here is no longer spotless, I thought I should tell you that too." He rubbed his hand across his face. "I felt terrible afterward but was afraid to admit to it. I'll pay the consequences and resign if that's what you and Blake want me to do."

"And the other things? Are you responsible for those

too?" *Here it comes. Blake was right.* I pressed my arms over my stomach.

"What other things? I've told you everything." He bent forward and clasped his hands in his lap. "Please believe me."

I exhaled a lengthy breath. "I believe you and I'll talk to Blake. One of us or Jocelyn will let you know what the consequences will be."

Wes stood and paused at the door. He turned back to me with a trembling chin and nodded.

~

Jocelyn said Wes could apologize to Robin, but it would be better if we scheduled an official meeting. She volunteered to set it up and follow through, for which I was grateful. At 10:30, I spoke positive messages to myself in preparation to visit Blake. I checked his calendar, and it appeared he was available.

I stopped at Tauni's desk to see if Blake was busy.

"You're always welcome to go in. He told me that this morning."

"This morning?" I glanced at Blake's open door and thanked Tauni. I closed his door behind me and took a seat in front of his desk.

He steepled his hands and waited for me to speak.

"We met with Wes." I filled Blake in on the details of our meeting and that Wes wanted to offer an apology to Robin.

"Anything else?" He relaxed back in his chair.

"Although this situation doesn't look good for Wes, I don't believe the vandalism involved him." I rubbed my hands together in my lap.

"I don't believe Wes was involved either."

"You don't?" I straightened. "Why not?"

"The police found prints in the greenhouse. Not Wes'. They didn't get any hits in their database."

"What? Why would his prints be in their database?"

"Years ago he worked for the government." He studied me with a blank expression. "Looks like you were right about him."

I shook my head. "How did you get results back so soon?"

"Matt's source at the police station pushed it through."

"I see. So, whose prints were they?" I crossed my legs and took a deep breath.

"They don't know yet. Police are still investigating. A couple of tools were stolen, which I doubt the police will mess with. But lucky for us, and unlucky for Hank, his wedding band was stolen."

"Your gardener's ring?"

"He often removes it when he works in the dirt. He forgot to pick it up when he left. That's why he came back later that afternoon." He chuckled. "He didn't want his wife to see him without his ring and think the worst."

I picked at my fingernails. "I can see where that could be misunderstood."

Blake crossed his arms and cringed. "No, 'I told you so' about Wes not being guilty?"

"You *were* right about Wes. Not me." I told him Wes confessed as the one who'd sabotaged Blake's presentation for the healthcare conference.

Blake cupped his hand over his chin. "What do we do now with that bit of information?"

"He's willing to resign, if that's what you want."

"Add this to his current violation and put him on official probation." He rose and strode to his conference table. "Please sit next to me here." He pointed to a chair at the table.

I stood and ambled to his side. My stomach rolled. "I need to get back to my office."

He let out a deep breath. "Did you review the form?"

"Still in my car." I gazed into Blake's eyes. "I don't get it. Why do we need a prenup? Do you suppose I'd try to rip you off if our marriage didn't work out?" I pulled a tissue from my skirt pocket. "Don't you realize I love you and not your money? We can work through anything as long as we trust in the Lord and have faith in one another."

"I should have told you about the prenup when I mentioned my estate plan. Please forgive me. I'm in turmoil over your not understanding my intentions. Review the stupid form, okay?"

~

After I arrived home that afternoon, I sat at my kitchen table and opened the folder to review the 'stupid' form. He named it correctly. He got high marks for that.

What I read shouldn't have surprised me, but I couldn't comprehend why, with his net worth, he worked a job. He didn't need one. He must find great satisfaction in his work. Besides his investments, his ranch did well, and his efforts to support musicians getting started in the industry appeared well-funded. Those two things should keep him busy enough. And he valued his home at almost four million dollars.

When I got to page three, all I could do was stare. *This makes little sense.* If we ended the marriage, I'd get fifty percent of his ranch, our new home, and a generous monthly support package. *Why would he do that?* I wasn't expecting anything like that if he died. His inheritance should go to his children. Not me. *He loves his ranch. Why would he . . .?*

I closed my eyes and groaned. *Oh, God, I'm sorry for being foolish. What does that man have to do, to make me feel secure, that he hasn't already done? You've given me an amazing man who loves me and wants the best for me, even if things go awry. He loves his ranch too much to give it up without a fight. Blake's a lot like You, Lord. He loves me and will sacrifice his all for me. Forgive me for not wanting to yield to his leadership and for my stubbornness. I submit to You and to Blake.*

Although I was hungry, I gathered the forms and hurried to my car.

Eighteen

I pulled my coat tighter around me and waited for Blake to answer his front door. I rang the bell again. The cool evening breeze flitted through my hair. *If he doesn't answer soon, I'll freeze. Maybe he's not home.* I turned toward my car, then twisted back to his door. *Dare I let myself inside? He said that was okay since I have the code.*

After I punched in the numbers and entered his foyer, I called out his name but received no response. I zipped into the kitchen to check the garage for his cars. I found all three vehicles. *He must be here somewhere but couldn't hear the doorbell.*

I walked through the main floor and called out his name. I took the back stairs up and roamed the second floor. No sign of him in his office, recording studio, theater room, or any of the bedrooms. I hurried down the front stairs and back to the kitchen, to the stairs that led to the basement. I'd never been there before but knew a little about it.

Worship music played somewhere down the long hallway. Storage areas were to my right and left, and a large open area lay ahead on my right. Blake's exercise room. I looked to my left and saw his sauna and hot tub.

Sound came from what I assumed was a bathroom. I took a few steps toward the door to call out Blake's name but stopped. *He's in the shower.*

This could embarrass us both if I wait for him here. I hurried up the stairs and sent him a text: I hope you don't mind, but I'm in your great room.

Blake came around the corner five minutes later. He wore dark jeans and a short sleeve, light blue tee. His wavy, salt and pepper gray hair hung damp across his forehead. He stared at me for a few seconds before he spoke. "Are we okay?"

I rushed to him and wrapped my arms around his neck. "I'm okay if you are."

Blake pulled away and gazed into my eyes. "You seem uptight over a lot of things. What's that about?"

"I'm experiencing trust issues, but the Lord's dealing with me on those. I'm sorry for my foolishness and understand what you wanted to show me in the form."

A hint of a smile appeared on his face. "And what was that?"

"You love your ranch and you'd do everything you could to keep it. Which means you'd do everything in your power to fight for our marriage."

He cupped my cheeks in his palms, kissed me, and drew me into a tight embrace. "I never want to let you go."

~

When Blake realized I hadn't eaten dinner, he invited me to stay. He said he'd check to see what his chef Richard had prepared, and he'd serve me.

"No, you won't. I'll help." I followed him to the refrigerator.

He glanced inside and brought out a covered casserole dish. After he peeked under the cover, he placed it back into the fridge. "Let's go out instead. How does pizza sound?"

"You ate pizza three days ago." I reopened the door. "What is it and why don't you want to serve it for dinner?" I pulled back the cover. "Richard's lasagna. I'd love to see why his is better than mine." I handed the dish to Blake. "Have at it, bubba."

"So, you've given me a pet name? Is that from a list on Google? Not too original if you ask me, lambchop."

I swatted his arm. "I'll come up with something more original than yours. You wait."

He laughed. "Let's warm the lasagna. I'm starving."

I found the plates, silverware, and glasses and set the table. Blake warmed our dinner and made garlic bread while I tossed a salad together and poured iced tea.

He offered a prayer of thanksgiving and waited for me to take the first bite.

"Oh my. This *is* amazing." I delved in again with my fork, savoring a mouthful of goodness. "You were right. I doubt I can compete. How often does he cook for you?"

"Four days a week. I'm on my own Friday through Sunday."

"I suppose I should cook those three days. Will he share his recipes with me, so we can eat this well all the time?" I served myself another helping.

Blake smiled. "Your Thanksgiving meal was sumptuous. You'll do fine without Richard's recipes."

I chuckled. "Have you been practicing that line since our last lasagna discussion?"

"I love your cooking." He smirked. "But we can eat out Friday through Sunday if needed." He winked.

"Funny."

After dinner, we returned to the great room.

Blake sat next to me on the sofa. "Are you ready to hear about my call with Andy?"

I nodded and snuggled into his arm.

"He answered my call Sunday evening and told me that he was struggling with our upcoming marriage, but he feels better about it now than he did." He lifted my chin. "That's progress."

"But what about a wedding date?"

He wrinkled his nose and narrowed his eyes. "I forgot to bring it up?"

I pulled away. "You forgot?"

"Don't be upset. He excited me when he answered his phone and talked with me. I'll try him again after you leave. Okay?"

I snuggled against his arm again. "No problem. Everything will work out." I stared up at Blake. "Let's call him now."

He dipped his head until his lips met mine. "March 2—six weeks from Saturday."

"But that's the anniversary week of Cheryl's death."

"A time of celebration and newfound joy in the uniting of two couples in marriage. If Andy weren't procrastinating, we could have made it sooner, but now we have little time before the baby's born." He pulled out his phone and looked at the calendar. "March 2 may not work. What if Zoey delivers two weeks early?" He peered at me.

"February 23 may work better." I stood and snatched my purse from the end table to use my cell's calendar. "And we should get them here a few weeks before that, so Zoey has time to find a doctor and get adjusted to her new surroundings."

"I hadn't thought about a doctor. That's a priority."

"Jenny talked to hers and he's taking new patients. I can give Zoey the information whenever she's ready."

"Do you think we can plan our wedding in five weeks?"

"With our daughters' help, we can do it." I smiled.

"Let me call Andy." Blake clicked on his son's number and relayed our plans. He told Andy that he wanted them to join us for a double wedding or at least be able to attend our ceremony on February 23.

He put his cell in his pocket. "I'm glad he's willing to talk, but I'm not sure he's ready to accept our union."

"I presume it's the salmon colored rose. Have you talked to him about that?"

"No. Are you ready to take another trip? I'd rather discuss that in person, and it would give you another opportunity to bond with Zoey."

"Will Allison be joining us?"

"We can ask her since that seems to be the only way I can get you there." His eyes twinkled.

~

We delighted Allison when we called and gave her our wedding date, and it thrilled her that we invited her to join us on our weekend trip. She rattled off all the things she wanted to do while in Albuquerque. Ride the tram up the Sandia Mountains, tour Old Town, and eat at her favorite restaurants. Blake told her that he doubted we'd do all those things, but he'd try to work at least one of them into our plans.

After he made our reservations, I drove home and enjoyed a peaceful night's rest.

On Wednesday, all seemed well in my life again.

But how long would that last? I chuckled as I climbed the stairs and entered my office.

Jocelyn poked her head inside my door. "I'm meeting with Wes and Robin this morning. I'll fill you in after."

"Sounds good, thanks." I opened my calendar and remembered this was my day to meet with Tauni for lunch. A highlight for sure. My schedule included two applicant interviews for an insurance specialist at 2:00 and 3:30. I planned to spend my time during the morning studying HR laws and policies.

I needed to talk to Blake again about leaving my position and finding another job. My heart wasn't in learning about HR, anyway. I disliked meeting with Robin and more so meeting with Wes, and I dreaded the thought of pouring over these HR manuals and studying online.

Blake stopped by during break time. "Hi, doll. Richard plans to prepare a roast today. Would you like to join me for dinner?"

"I'm no doll, but that sounds great."

Blake shook his head. "I'll stop by and pick you up at 6:30."

I gave him a thumbs up.

For lunch, Tauni and I walked to a barbeque place. She greeted everyone we met along the way.

I glanced at her from the corner of my eye and nudged her elbow. "Why are you doing that? You've never done that before."

"I love to say hello to strangers now. Maybe it's weird, but I want them to know someone cares about them."

"That's sweet."

"No big deal." She shrugged. "I often imagined no one cared about me, but when someone smiled or said, good morning, my day went better."

"I hope you didn't feel that way often." We entered the restaurant and waited to be seated. "We're all special and important to God."

Tauni nodded. "I understand now, but sometimes I still struggle."

"Please reach out to me during those times. I'm here for you."

After we ordered our lunch, she said, "Blake *is* the best boss. I like working with him."

"I'm glad you're enjoying yourself. Has he asked you to do anything you've found challenging?" There were many times he pushed me to where I struggled to keep my cool.

"No, but he asked me to redo the file room. He said he has a hard time finding what he's looking for in there. Did he ever mention that to you?"

After they delivered our food, I chuckled. "I rearranged things. He didn't like it, but I never changed it back." I salted my French fries. "Now. Tell me all about Quade."

She sighed. "He's wonderful. Sweet. An exceptional kisser." She covered her mouth. Her eyes sparkled.

"You're too funny. I'm glad things are going well."

"We have dinner dates planned for tomorrow and Friday, bowling and a movie on Saturday, church on Sunday, and I'm meeting him at the ranch again next Monday for lunch."

I raised my eyebrows. "You might want to slow down a little."

"Probably, but I'm crazy about him. I want us to spend every free minute together and think he feels the same way. I couldn't be happier."

"Please be careful." I moved my hand across the table toward her. "Remember, it's only been two weeks."

She leaned toward me. "Thanks for your concern, but I'm sure he's the one. The Lord has answered my prayers." She stabbed her fries with her fork. "How does Blake show his love for you?"

"He shows his love through gifts like the roses and wanting to spend time with me." I grinned and looked toward the windows. "He loves to hold my hand and be close. He says sweet things to me, and sometimes he does something special for me like making me a café mocha."

"You forgot one of the biggest ones."

"What did I leave out?"

"The way he lights up when you enter the room. You've captivated his heart. Of that I'm certain."

Warmth spread up my neck and cheeks. "He does do that, doesn't he?"

Nineteen

After lunch, I poked my head inside Jocelyn's door. "How did your meeting go this morning with Wes and Robin?"

"I meant to stop by. Been a wild day." She stood and stepped toward me. "Everything went well. Wes got a little emotional when he talked with her. He seemed to feel bad about it."

"How did Robin respond?"

"She felt bad too. She told me afterward she thought of him as a lovesick puppy." Jocelyn grinned. "I reminded them both of the policy that states people in the same department cannot date."

"Why did you need to tell Robin? She wanted nothing to do with him."

"After he apologized, she told him that she was sorry she caused him trouble. At one point I thought she might hug him. If it weren't for the policy, I think she'd agree to lunch at least."

"Oh, my."

"We must monitor this situation."

I nodded. "And I need to ask for Friday off again this week."

"Where are you and Blake off to this time?" She

smiled.

"Albuquerque to visit his son." I turned to leave and spoke over my shoulder. "His daughter is traveling with us again."

"No explanations are necessary."

~

That evening, Blake picked me up after work and drove me to his place. We chatted while he warmed dinner. "Was Jenny excited we set a date?"

"I'll call her now so you can listen."

He spun and faced me. "You forgot to call your daughter and tell her, didn't you?"

I chuckled. "I've been busy, and I wanted to share her excitement with you."

"You picked on me for not talking to Andy about setting a date, and you haven't told Jenny we set one?"

"I'll put her on speaker." I tried to hide my grin, placed my phone on the kitchen counter, and clicked on Jenny's number. We listened to three rings. "Hi, Nana. Can I talk to Papa?"

"What about talking to me?"

Blake laughed. "Hi, giggly girl."

Nicki giggled. "Hi, precious papa."

I shook my head. "Let me talk to Mommy."

"Okay. M O M M Y, it's Nana." I backed away from the phone and rubbed my ears.

Jenny greeted me, and we chatted about Nicki for a minute.

"We set our date for February 23."

"Yeah, I heard from Allison this morning." Sarcasm laced her voice. "Thanks for sharing that important news with me right away, Mom."

"I'm sorry, Jen. Time got away from me today."

"I'm happy for you and Blake and hope Andy and Zoey will join you."

"We're flying out there this weekend to visit in person and hope they'll commit." I pulled plates from the overhead cabinet. "You're the wedding expert, what should we do first?"

She rattled a paper. "The first thing you should do is contact Manuel to see if he's available that day and time. Are you getting married at the church or somewhere else?"

I peered at Blake. "The church?"

"We could have it here at my house unless you prefer the church."

Jenny said, "Beautiful. Mom descending the stairs and waltzing into the foyer. Breathtaking."

I shook my head. "I'm not sure about breathtaking, but Blake's foyer would be a lovely location for a wedding."

"After you get that figured out, you need to stop by and confirm the order at the stationery store and give them the date and time. We must get the invitations back soon so we can get them addressed and mailed out right away."

"Wait, a minute. Confirm the order?"

"Allison and I got together on Monday and picked out invitations we thought you might like, but you can change them. We ordered our dresses on Tuesday, and Allison texted a picture of a maternity dress to Zoey we felt she might like. I don't know if Allison's heard from her yet."

"Wow." I glanced at Blake. "Our daughters are amazing planners."

He smiled. "What about Nicki? We'll want her as

our flower girl."

"She'll love that. I'll take her shopping this weekend."

"Great. Anything else?" I asked.

"Allison said she'd order the flowers and believed Blake would line up musicians and have his chef prepare the reception food. Does that work?"

Blake agreed. "Thanks for jumping in and being ready to move on this."

Jenny chuckled. "The least I can do. You're doing me a big favor by taking care of Mom and relieving me of that immense burden. I owe you my sanity."

Blake tilted his head back and laughed. "She can be difficult, can't she?"

I placed my hands on my hips and took a firm stance. "Enough, you two."

~

After dinner and kitchen duty, Blake took me on a tour of the attic. The only floor I hadn't seen. "When you pack your things, you can store them here until we move into the new house." He pointed to an available space much larger than I needed.

I nodded and looked at Blake. "When Andy and Zoey move to Nashville, they'll need most of my things. I'll pack up all personal items but leave my cookware, dishes, utensils, and those types of things for them in the condo."

Blake turned toward me. "I'm sure they'll appreciate that."

"I have a trunk in the guest room I'd like to keep. Sam's mother passed it down to him." I stared off into a corner of the room. "He kept his toys and belongings inside of it for years. Nicki calls it her treasure chest." I got quiet and stammered. "Now might be an excellent time to pass it along to Jenny." I gazed at Blake, my eyes wide.

He wrapped his arms around me. "You should keep it. Nicki will enjoy finding it in our new house. We can put it in the recreation room or on the upper floor where she can fill it with her treasures for years to come."

We walked further down the hallway to an area at the other end of the attic. Several easels covered with cloths lined the walls. Blake removed the covering on one to show me one of Cheryl's unfinished projects of a lovely landscape. After he replaced the cloth, he suggested I look at her other artwork if interested when we moved my personal things upstairs.

He took my hand. "Ready to relax by the fireplace?"

We strolled into the great room. Blake played soft music through his home speaker system and we settled on the couch.

His arm rested along the back of the sofa. "Are you looking forward to our trip?"

"I look forward to being with you." I stared into Blake's eyes and winked.

"Are you telling me the entire truth?"

I leaned away and gaped at him. "What do you mean? I'll admit, our working together and living together may be hard on both of us, but I love to spend time with you."

"Jocelyn told me that you're having a hard time adjusting to your new position."

"Jocelyn has a big mouth." I focused on my hands in my lap.

"Don't get upset with her. I asked and she shared." He lifted my chin. "I want more than anything for you to be happy."

I avoided his eyes. "Tuesday was horrible. That was my fault, but to go into the office and act like everything was fine when I felt my world had crashed down around me was tough. And to know you were right around the corner made it harder because I wasn't ready to face you."

"If you suppose working together at the same place could lead to extra difficulties for us, I'm in favor of you looking elsewhere for a job."

I glanced at Blake. "Great." I kissed his cheek.

"Nope." He pointed to his lips. "Right here, penguin."

"Penguin?"

"They must be the cutest animal in the world. Fits you well."

"Sweet, but I don't think so. Wear a black tux with a white shirt for our wedding and I'll call *you* penguin instead."

His face turned serious. "I've wanted to ask you something. I remembered it upstairs when you mentioned Sam."

"Go ahead."

"Did Sam die at home?"

I shook my head and looked toward the windows. "The hospital. He'd been waiting on a heart transplant."

"I shouldn't ask you these tough questions. But I know we share similar pain."

"You can ask me anything." I peered into his eyes.

Blake frowned. "Were you with him when he died?"

I closed my eyes and took a deep breath. "I'd gone to the cafeteria with Carl. Jenny stayed with Sam. He passed while I was away."

"I'm sure that was tough." He squeezed my hand. "I'm bothered that Cheryl didn't have anyone with her when she died."

"But she did." I reached up and wiped a tear from the side of his face. "The Lord was with her."

"Thank you for reminding me of that." He placed his arm across my shoulder and pulled me closer. After a few minutes of silence, he said, "You sure are snuggly."

I gazed into his blue eyes and smiled. "Snuggly. Snuggles. I like it."

"Do you mean we found a pet name you approve of?"

"Was it on your list?"

He nodded.

"Then keep trying."

Twenty

Albuquerque, New Mexico

Friday, Blake, Allison, and I picked up our rental car, a Nissan Maxima, and drove to Andy and Zoey's apartment.

Blake asked if I'd contacted Andy or Zoey to let them know we were coming to town. I wrinkled my nose. *Now I'm his personal assistant regarding his family?* Blake then said he tried to contact Andy but hadn't heard back. Allison and I both texted Zoey, but she never got back with us either.

We chatted about our wedding plans during our drive from the airport. I told Blake and Allison that Manuel was available to perform the weddings, but we needed to talk to him soon about the details. Allison asked about the invitations, and I told her I wanted to wait before I confirmed them because I expected to include Andy and Zoey's names.

We pulled to the curb on their street and all got out in front of a graffiti covered, white block wall. They lived in a small terracotta stucco apartment on the far right.

Blake rushed to my side. "Let me help you."

Allison shook her head and looked at me. "Why does Dad need to help you?"

"Because I'm a southern gentleman." He chuckled and dipped his head. "At your service ma'am." He reached out his hand to me.

I told Allison about my childhood in a poor neighborhood and how my first visit to Albuquerque brought back many unpleasant memories. "I think that's the actual reason your dad wanted to help me, but I'm doing better this time. Thanks." I smiled at Blake.

"I have a thoughtful father." She grinned and pointed to the building. "Apartment C?"

Blake and I nodded, and Allison hurried through the wrought-iron gate, across the sandy front yard, and knocked on the door.

The curtain, covering the barred window, pulled back and dropped. Allison stood on the front step, and after a red-eyed Zoey swung the door open, she hugged Allison's neck. When she saw Blake and me behind Allison, she sobbed and gathered us in a group hug. "He's gone again. Been three days this time."

Blake ran his fingers through his hair. "But I talked to him on Tuesday evening."

Zoey pulled us inside out of the wind. "He took off right after your call. I haven't heard from him since." She rubbed her baby belly and grimaced. "He took my car and my phone."

I touched her on her shoulder. "Did he say anything when he left?"

Zoey padded to the sofa and invited us to sit. In addition to the couch, the small living room held one old chair, an end table with a lamp, and an older model television. "Sounded to me that his conversation with

Blake went well. He hung up and told me that you wanted to get married on February 23. He said he was going for a drive to think and we'd talk it over when he came home."

Blake sat next to Zoey. "Did he take anything else with him?"

"Only my cell. I'd been to see my doctor and forgot to bring it inside with me. I'm tempted to look at it when I drive, so I put it in the glove box." She covered her face with her hands and lowered her head.

Blake rose and walked over to Allison and me where we stood near the front door. "I don't like this. Something's happened to him. I'll call Luis to report a missing person."

Luis Ortiz, a friend of Blake's, was a police officer in Albuquerque. He had helped Blake locate Andy in November when we were in town for a healthcare conference.

Allison gnawed at her lower lip and sat on one side of Zoey rubbing her back. I sat on the other side and did my best to console her for the next hour, while Blake paced across the living room.

When Luis arrived, Zoey told him everything she remembered.

Luis looked at Blake. "Since he's over eighteen, there's not much we can do. Doesn't sound like a crime has been committed. He may have skipped town for unknown reasons." He glanced at Zoey. "However, if you report your car as stolen, we can have him arrested for theft when we locate him."

Zoey jumped up. "Arrested? He'd hate me if I did that to him." She shook her head. "No."

Blake placed his hands on her shoulders. "Let's give

him some time. There's probably a good reason for his absence." He turned toward me—his eyebrows pinched together.

Luis completed his report, shook Blake's hand, and said goodbye to Allison and Zoey.

He approached me last. "I see there's a ring on your finger. I knew what I saw in November was admiration and affection." Luis strode to the front door and opened it.

He turned back to Zoey. "You still own an old brown Sentra, right?"

She nodded.

"Looks like Andy just came home."

~

Andy shoved past Luis, scanned the living room, and focused on Zoey where she stood near the hallway that led to the bedroom. "I'm sorry. I promise it won't happen again." He took a step closer, but she backed away.

"That's what you said last time. And you know what? You're right. I won't let it happen again." She rushed past Andy and over to where Blake stood near the front door. She grasped his arm. "Please take me home to Nashville when you go back." Tears streamed down her face. "Please?"

Andy squished his eyebrows together and frowned. He spoke to us in a pleading tone. "May I have a few minutes alone with Zoey?"

Luis opened the front door, and the rest of us hurried toward it.

Zoey followed us but spoke to Andy. "No. I don't want to be alone with you. Say whatever you have to say to all of us."

Andy shook his head. "I texted and called you every day." His chin trembled. "I didn't realize until three hours ago that your cell was in the glove box." He stepped toward her and this time she didn't retreat. "I got here as fast as I could. I was working in Las Cruces."

"You left to take a drive, in my car, and ended up on a job in Las Cruces? That's over 200 miles from here." She placed her fists on her hips. "I don't believe you."

He pulled a cell out of his pocket and handed it to Zoey. "All here in the texts and voicemails."

I glanced at Blake. "Deja Vu?"

Allison wrinkled her nose. I guess she hadn't heard the story about me being locked in her dad's garage.

Zoey's eyes darted around the room. She seemed confused. Uncertain.

I took her by the hand. "Could we talk in your room?"

Luis told everyone goodbye, and Blake followed him out. Allison ambled to the sofa and sat, while Andy gazed at Zoey. Zoey lowered her eyes and led me to her bedroom.

I closed her door behind me. "You might want to read the texts and listen to the voicemails before you respond to Andy again."

She peered at her phone and sat on her bed. I leaned my back against her closet door to give her space.

After she'd clicked on her texts and listened to her voicemails, she peeked at me. "Like he said. He told me that he'd gotten a job offer from the friend he'd gone to visit when he left here on Tuesday. They needed to leave right away."

I took a seat next to her.

She rose and sighed. "If I needed transportation, he

told me to contact his friend's girlfriend. She offered to take me wherever I needed to go." She spun toward me with tears in her eyes. "He texted me every day to check on me and told me in every text and phone call that he loved me and he'd see me soon."

I stood, embraced her, and chuckled.

She pulled back and stared at me with her mouth opened. "Are you laughing at me?"

"I suffered a similar incident with Blake the day you and Andy flew home after the engagement party." I told her about our argument, that I'd spent time in Blake's garage, and how Blake and Jenny tried to call and text me. "These phones are great when you remember to keep them with you." I grinned.

"What did you do? I feel foolish for getting upset when he planned to make sure I was okay."

"I forgave Blake for getting upset and leaving me. Although, I continue on most days to remain foolish." I smiled. "Andy loves you, Zoey. Believe and accept it."

She pursed her lips. "I guess I'd better accept his apology and tell him and everyone else who experienced my outburst I'm sorry too."

~

Zoey took Andy's hand and apologized with tears in her eyes to him and the rest of the family. After she received a hug from Andy, we went to dinner at Luis's brother's restaurant. I'd met Juan Ortiz in November also.

When we arrived, Blake asked the hostess if Juan could join us for dinner. He wasn't available but told me that he'd order plenty of green chili for our table. He knew I wasn't a fan, but he loved to tease.

Blake and I sat on one side of a booth, Zoey and

Andy on the other, and Allison took a seat at the end of the table. We devoured chips and salsa while we waited on our food order to arrive. While Allison and Andy chatted about our visit with Debra and Augusta, Zoey excused herself to the restroom. Allison followed her.

Blake seemed quiet. He fidgeted with his fork in one hand while he bounced his knee.

Andy peered across the table at me. He opened his mouth to speak. Stopped and looked down at his placemat.

I cleared my throat. "Would have been great to have you with us in Florida. I hope we can do it again soon and have you and Zoey join us."

Andy lifted his eyes. "Did you enjoy meeting Grandmother?"

"I did. We seemed to hit it off well."

"Based on her calls to me, I'd say you did." He glanced toward the hostess when she strolled by. "Last night, Allison called me and tricked me into calling her back."

Blake said, "What did she do?"

"She left me a message that sounded urgent. 'Call me right away. I've got to tell you what's happened. Please Andy. I must talk with you now.' She scared me into thinking you had an accident."

I tilted my head. "What did she say when you called her?"

He raised the pitch of his voice to sound like a girl. "You need to get that chip off your shoulder and accept Keedryn as Dad's wife. He was miserable before she came around, grumpy since Mom's death. You sure didn't help things by running off either. She's a wonderful woman, and you should welcome her like

Grandmother and I have."

I held back a giggle. I imagined Allison saying those exact words to her little brother. "Andy, I do hope we can be friends."

He stared at the table.

Blake laid his hand on Andy's. "Son, I want to apologize for giving Keedryn one of your mother's favorite roses. I should have been more sensitive about the color I chose. If I offended you, I'm sorry."

Andy shook his head. "That's not the whole issue, Dad."

Twenty-one

Blake opened his mouth to speak but stopped. Juan motioned for him to come over to where he stood. "Excuse me, I'll be back."

Andy kept his eyes down. I moved my hand across the table to get his attention. He leaned back in his seat, glanced up at me, and narrowed his eyes.

I swallowed hard. "When your dad told me I was his one-and-only, he didn't mean I was the only one he'd ever loved. I can't speak for him, but when my husband died, my life as I knew it ended. I adored Sam and never expected love to come again."

Andy sighed and closed his eyes.

I spoke with as much compassion as I could. "But on Christmas evening, after your dad sent you and the rest of the family inside the house, and before I drove away, I told him he'd become my one-and-only."

Andy picked up his paper napkin and twisted it around his fingers.

"I love your dad. Marrying him doesn't mean I'll forget Sam. He'll always hold a special place in my heart. And I'm sure your dad feels the same way about your mother."

Andy stared at his napkin and shredded it.

I rubbed my hands together underneath the table. *Help me get through to him, Lord.* "Andy. Please look at me."

His eyes met mine and he rubbed his bottom lip.

"I assume that when your dad said I was his one-and-only, and you overheard him at the engagement party, that's what he meant too." I sat back and tried to get a sense of what Andy was feeling.

He squeezed his eyes closed again and opened them. "How did you know that's what bothered me?"

I tilted my head. "Let's call it women's intuition."

Zoey pressed into her seat next to Andy.

Allison plopped into her chair and wiped her brow. "Whew. That took us a long time. Juan caught us when we came out of the restroom and asked if it was true that you and Dad got engaged. He made me take his address and promise him an invitation." Allison giggled. "He's telling Dad now. We'll be in so much trouble if we don't invite him and Luis."

Blake returned soon after they delivered three enchilada dinners, one taco dinner, and my chicken quesadilla to our table. "If we forget him, I don't think he'll forgive us." He chuckled. "And he wants to send home a quart of green chili with Keedryn. He said she needs to develop a taste for it."

Juan watched us from a distance, and I raised my hand and waved.

Allison grinned. "I'm starving. Who's going to say the blessing?"

"I will." Andy bowed his head. "Father, we thank you for this food and your blessings all around us. I thank you for Zoey, the love of my life. And I'm happy you brought Keedryn into Dad's life too. Bless their marriage and ours. Amen."

I glanced at Blake, who eyed Andy.

When I looked across the table at Andy, he said to Blake, "Keedryn explained the one-and-only conversation I overheard. She made sense." He took a bite of his enchilada.

Zoey rubbed Andy's arm. "That was sweet. Your prayer and what you said about Keedryn."

He gazed into her eyes. "Thanks." A blush moved up to his cheeks.

After an enjoyable dinner, we drove Zoey and Andy back to their apartment.

Before they climbed out of the car, Blake said, "Talk about what you want to do regarding the wedding on February 23 and moving back to Nashville. We'd love to have you, but we'll understand if you stay here in Albuquerque. We can talk about this more tomorrow."

Blake took us to our hotel where Allison and I agreed earlier to share a room. When we got into the elevator, she pushed the button to our floor. "Zoey wants to move, what do you think Andy wants to do."

After the doors opened, Blake led the way down the hallway. "I'm not sure Andy knows the answer to that question yet."

~

After breakfast on Saturday, the three of us went to Andy and Zoey's apartment. Blake and I agreed to not bring up the move or wedding until later that afternoon. With a high of forty-six degrees and sunshine, we walked around Old Town visiting art galleries, shops, an old church, and ate lunch in a restaurant there.

Back at Andy and Zoey's home, Zoey asked if we'd like something to drink. I agreed to help. After we took everyone's drink order, I followed Zoey into the kitchen and Allison slipped into the bathroom.

"Has Andy said anything yet about the wedding next month?"

Zoey sounded hopeful. "I think he's ready to commit. With what he said last night at dinner, and how he seemed to enjoy our morning, I hope he'll say yes and mean it this time."

"Blake just said something to him. Let's hurry and get these drinks ready." I grabbed the ice cube trays and filled the glasses Zoey placed in front of me. She added water to three of them and cola to the others. We rushed out to the living room and distributed the drinks.

Andy rubbed his face. "I'm good now." He reached for Zoey's hand. "If my bride-to-be wants to move to Nashville and get married there, I'm ready."

"Sweet." Zoey bent down to hug Andy's neck, tipped her glass of ice water, and drenched him.

Andy shot up out of his chair. "Man, that's cold."

"I'm so sorry." Zoey ran to the kitchen and brought back a handful of paper towels.

Andy wrapped her in his arms. "Don't worry. I'll dry off. Not a problem."

I winked at Blake and mouthed. "You trained him right."

Blake smiled and focused on Andy. "How soon do you want to move?"

"I must get back to Las Cruces tomorrow so I'm ready to work on Monday. This job's big and pays a lot more than the other ones I've worked. I can't be late."

"Son, quit and come home. You can load your car and be in Nashville in two or three days. You'll be able to find work there."

"I can't. I gave Chip my word I'd finish this job."

Zoey spoke in a frustrated tone. "When will that be?"

"Three more weeks."

Zoey opened her eyes wide. "How often will you get home?"

"I'll come back on Friday nights and leave Sunday afternoons."

She pouted. "I don't like it."

I stood. "But that should work. We have five weeks until the wedding. Gives Andy and Zoey two weeks to get to Nashville after his job ends. That's enough time."

Allison shook her head. "That's too close if you ask me."

Andy cut her a look. "No one did, sis."

Zoey peeked at Blake and me. "I don't want to stay here for three weeks without him." She peered at Andy. "I'd like to fly back with your family and get settled. If that's okay with you."

Andy frowned and focused on Zoey. "If that's what you want." He stared at the floor. "Be good for you to find a doctor and get situated and to help with plans for the wedding too." He sighed and looked at Blake. "Is that okay, Dad?"

Blake agreed and we initiated our plan. Zoey would return to Nashville with us the following morning and after Andy's job ended, he'd join us. We left them to pack Zoey's things for her trip and to spend quality time together before their separation. Since they rented the apartment furnished, Andy would bring the rest of their belongings by car because they didn't have much.

I prayed his job would end in time for the wedding.

Twenty-two

Late January
Nashville, Tennessee

We arrived in Nashville at 4:50 Sunday afternoon and at my condo at 6:20. Blake reminded me when he dropped Zoey and me off that he'd be out of the office the following day for the executives' off-site winter workshop.

As soon as we stepped inside my condo, Zoey took a tour. Her excitement was contagious. "This is where I get to live? Andy and I together?" She clapped her hands. "I love it."

"Not as fancy as Blake's house, but I've enjoyed living here." I smiled.

"I wouldn't want to live there. To me, this is a big mansion." Zoey padded to each room, with her hand pressed against her lower back, and glowed. She stared into the guest room. "Is this my room?"

I nodded. "I have to leave at 7:30 in the morning to get to work on time. The keys to my old car will be on the kitchen counter if you need to go anywhere. Call if you need me."

"Do you mind if I relax and watch TV?" She ambled

into my TV room while I fixed us a light dinner of ham and cheese sandwiches.

After our meal, Zoey called Andy and talked to him while I unpacked. She squealed as she told him about their new home. The home I'd shared with Sam the last two years of his life.

~

Monday morning, I slipped out early, hoping Zoey would sleep in and get much needed rest after her trip to her new home. When I arrived at the office, I prepared my second resignation letter within a month. Better for me not to have to learn a new career while adjusting to married life. I sensed peace about the decision and believed God led me to this moment.

A file cabinet drawer opened and closed in Jocelyn's office. I carried in my letter to let her know of my decision.

"Great. You're here." She grinned. "I need to take this file to the winter workshop. Did Blake already go?"

"He must have gone from home because I haven't seen him this morning." I inched my way closer to her desk. "Thank you for the opportunity, but I feel it's best for me to leave."

Her expression faded when I handed her my letter. "I'm disappointed but not all that surprised."

"I'll help for up to four weeks if needed. But I'd like to leave before the week of my wedding."

She agreed and asked me to put together a job listing for the position and get it posted because she'd be out for the rest of the day. She said goodbye and rushed out the door.

I worked on the job posting and several other tasks to get caught up from taking Friday off. So much to do,

I didn't notice it was noon until Tauni called my cell.

She sounded frantic. "Did you know Blake is having your tree removed today?"

"My tree?" I jumped up. "What?"

"Quade invited me for lunch at the ranch. We're having a picnic in his pickup near your new homesite."

"Slow down. I'm having trouble understanding."

"No time to slow down. They're here clearing out trees along the road for a new driveway to your house. They're almost finished but getting ready to chop down your tree too."

"On my way. Stall them." *Not my tree. Lord, please stop them. Get me there on time.*

I drove faster than I should have and made it to the dirt road that ran in front of the ranch in fifteen minutes. When I pulled down the long and winding driveway, men and their equipment stood near my tree. I jumped out of my car and ran as fast as I could.

"Wait," I shouted. "There's been a mistake. You can't cut down this tree."

The crew looked at me like I was crazy. One of the men pulled out the work order and handed it to me. "Sorry, lady. This tree's gotta go."

"A mistake. Not this tree."

"Lady. Definitely this tree." He motioned to another man. "Let's get this done."

I knew I couldn't call Blake. If he were eating, it would be a working lunch, and he'd have his phone off.

The work crew brought their equipment into position, which left me no other choice. I reached up to the lowest limb, grabbed ahold, hoisted myself up, and took a seat. I prayed I wouldn't fall.

The men cussed at me and called me a lunatic. The

worker who'd insisted the tree must come down, called someone on his cell. He must have been told to leave, because he and his crew moved their equipment out and away.

Thankful they gave up, I attempted to find a way out of the tree. Tauni and Quade were nearby but laughed so hard they could barely stand.

After I called out for help, Quade rushed over and helped me down. "Careful now. Blake will fire me if something happens to you."

When I landed, I glanced at Tauni standing a few feet away. "What are you doing?"

Smiling, Tauni strolled toward me. "I videotaped the entire thing to share on social media."

"Some friend you are." I had to admit, if it were anyone other than me, I would have enjoyed viewing it on social media too. "You'd better edit that before you post it."

Blake called me during his break and sounded upset. "What happened? I got a voicemail from the tree cutters saying you climbed that ugly tree and refused to come down."

My body tensed. "I'll fill you in when I see you."

"Fill me in now. I paid them a lot of money to cut down those trees."

I pulled my cell away from my ear and stared at it. *What is his problem?* I brought the phone back to my ear, my voice firm. "But I love that tree."

"Then why didn't you tell me about this before? I wouldn't have paid them to cut it down if I knew it meant so much to you."

Paid them? "You're worried about your money?" I inhaled a deep breath and let it out. "Send me a bill. I'll reimburse you."

His tone softened but remained brusque. "K, you're too old to climb trees."

"Quade came to my rescue and helped me down."

He sighed. "Now I'll need to give him a raise for adding to his ranch responsibilities. He needs to look after my wife and keep her out of trouble." He huffed. "Jenny was right. You *are* a tremendous burden."

He's impossible. "Funny." I hung up without saying goodbye.

Later that afternoon Blake viewed Tauni's post and called me again with another scolding. But then he laughed at the hilarity of it. "I'm glad you're safe, but that video could go viral."

Still annoyed over his first scolding, I sounded agitated. "I'm in good shape for a middle-aged woman, so you need not worry about me."

"K, I love you. Please be careful."

I softened my tone. "Was rather humorous, wasn't it?"

He cleared his throat. "On a serious note, I received a voicemail from Matt Starnes and plan to call him as soon as we hang up. He has news regarding the investigation into Eliza's death."

"Did he share any details?"

"Just that they ruled it accidental."

I brought my hand to my chest. "Such a relief."

"I'll find out more and we'll talk later." We disconnected our call.

On my way home, I stopped by the stationery store and confirmed the perfect wedding invitations that Jenny and Allison picked out. I paid for an expedited order and shipment. They guaranteed we'd receive them by the following Monday. If we could get them addressed and to the post office by that Saturday, the invites would be in the mail three weeks before the wedding.

After Zoey and I ate our dinner of homemade chicken noodle soup and fresh bread rolls, I taped together a few boxes I'd stored and packed books and knickknacks.

Zoey offered to help. "I look forward to our weddings and to become Mrs. Andrew Conner. I'm happy we'll marry before the baby's born."

"Me too." I handed her bubble wrap for the breakable items. "Did you get back with Allison about the dress photo she texted to you?"

"She ordered it for me." Her voice rose an octave. "Should be here by Friday."

"Mine should be here this week too. We should model them for each other."

We giggled and teased one another as though we'd known each other for years until she got a call from her sweetheart. All her attention went to Andy. They talked for over an hour, and she turned in for the night.

Blake called before I got ready for bed and told me that he'd spoken to his attorney and knew what happened to Eliza, but he wanted to tell me in person. He had an early meeting with the executive team, so breakfast was out. We agreed to have lunch the following day.

After his call, I spent time with my journal and Bible. With Eliza's death behind us and plans in place for a double wedding, I felt at peace. No more stress about my job, my tree was safe, and I bonded with Zoey. *Thank you, Lord, for a good day.*

Twenty-three

Tuesday, Blake and I drove to Franklin for lunch at a French restaurant.

I sat to his right at a table near the front windows. We helped ourselves to the soup and salad bar after we placed our order. When we returned to our seats, I said, "Don't keep me in suspense any longer. What happened to Eliza?"

"From what Matt learned, the park ranger saw her around 5:00 p.m. standing along the edge of the lake while he was making his rounds before the park closed. He told her that she needed to leave."

I scooted closer to Blake. I didn't want to miss any details.

"Eliza turned away from him and ran toward the East parking area. He followed her to make sure she made it to her car. He said she was exhibiting odd behavior."

"That lines up with her actions when I talked with her." I ate a spoonful of my French onion soup.

"He caught up with her, escorted her to her car, and wrote down her license plate number."

The waitress placed glasses of water on our table and slipped away.

Blake took a drink. "She drove off, and he returned to the West entrance where his car was parked and prepared to leave for the night. On his way out, he decided to check the East entrance to make sure she hadn't returned to the area." He took a bite of his salad.

"Oh my. She must have been acting odd when she drove off too."

Blake nodded. "The ranger found her car parked in a driveway on Otter Creek Road. He reentered the park and searched the tree line next to the road that runs along the lake where he'd seen her earlier."

"I've been there, I know what road you're talking about."

Blake leaned closer and lowered his voice. "He found her soon after 6:00. Appears she rolled down the embankment, bumped her head on a tree stump, and landed with her face in the water."

"Oh, Blake. How awful." I covered my mouth with my hand. "But why did the police need to question all of us if it was an accident?"

"Standard investigation to make sure, I guess. Although the park ranger didn't notice anyone else, her actions were strange, and the police wanted to make sure no one followed her there."

"Poor Cindy." I shook my head. "But now she knows her mother's death was an accident and not murder."

"That must be a relief for her."

"And I hope it brings her peace."

~

I looked forward to Wednesday's lunch with Tauni. Her relationship with Quade appeared to be growing fast. *Maybe faster than mine and Blake's.* We met outside my office and strolled to a nearby deli.

After we placed our order, I asked, "How many times have you and Quade been together since lunch at the ranch on Monday?"

"Monday and Tuesday for dinner." She grinned and fiddled with her spoon. "He's taking me to Samson's on Friday. That's where Blake took you in December, isn't it?"

"And where he first kissed me. Then after he took me home, he told me that he loved me."

"Oh." Her smile faded. "What if Quade tells me that he loves me?"

I tilted my head. "Isn't that what you want?"

She touched her neck. "Yes, but no. Not yet." She glanced around her and back at me. "I need to tell him things first. I don't want to hear him say, 'I love you,' and have him walk away."

"What are you talking about?" I grasped her fingers in my hand. "Why would he leave you?"

She whispered, "Because of my past. I must tell him first. Afterward, if he tells me that he loves me, I'll know he truly does."

"God has forgiven you for everything. Read Romans 8. Your past shouldn't make any difference in Quade's feelings for you."

"That's what I need to be sure of. I must tell him everything before Friday."

~

Tauni plodded down the hall toward my office on Friday morning with a blank expression on her face. She knocked, stepped inside, and spoke in a somber tone. "He broke off tonight's date. And tomorrow's and the next day's too." She slumped into the chair.

"I don't know what to say. I never expected this from him."

She stared at the floor. "I can't blame him. I have more baggage than the carousel at the airport." A tear slid down her cheek. "I'm not marriage material." She stood and rushed out my door before I could say another word.

I rose to follow her to her office. *Men. What's wrong with them? Quade should know what the Bible says about forgiveness. Has he never sinned? How could he do this to her?*

Blake stopped me in the hallway. "Tauni's in tears at her desk. I don't know what to do with her."

I filled him in on how Quade broke her heart.

"That doesn't sound like Quade. After he takes time to think this through, I expect he'll change his mind and see he made a rash decision. Let's give him a chance."

~

After a few minutes with Tauni, I returned to my office and reviewed resumes for my HR position. Certain Jocelyn would scan my top picks, I ambled into her office to share my findings. "I found four exceptional HR generalist candidates. Please look them over and I'll make calls later this afternoon to schedule their interviews for next week." I placed printed copies on her desk.

"Great. I'll get them back to you soon."

An hour later I made the calls, conducted short phone interviews with three of the candidates, and scheduled their interviews for the following week. I left a message for the fourth one to contact me.

When I arrived home that evening, Zoey wore her blue wedding dress.

"You look amazing. Andy won't be able to take his eyes off you."

She smiled. "I guess with me over eight months pregnant, no one will take their eyes off me."

I laughed and opened my package which also arrived. After I slipped on my lavender and deep purple dress, Zoey and I stared at ourselves in my full-length bedroom mirror. "We look good."

We hugged each other and called Allison and Jenny to tell them the dresses fit well.

After dinner, Blake called to let me know that he wouldn't be able to take Zoey and me to the ranch in the morning. "Let's make it around 4:00 in the afternoon. I plan to work at the ranch with Quade most of the day."

"Good. Talk sense into that man," I said, while tapping my finger on my kitchen counter.

"I'll do what I can but give him time." He chuckled and we ended our call.

I sat at the kitchen table with a cup of tea and thought about Tauni while Zoey relaxed in the tub. I picked up my cell and clicked on Tauni's number.

She sounded gloomy. I hated for her to be alone all weekend. I knew that feeling. To be in love, think you're loved in return, only to have the one you love walk away. That was me one month earlier. I sighed. God turned Blake and my situation around. He could do that for Tauni and Quade too. *If it's His will.*

I invited her to join Zoey and me in the morning in the guise of baking cookies. But more so to offer encouragement and love.

Tauni agreed to arrive at my place at 9:00 a.m. and thanked me for caring about her. I intended to get her mind off Quade for a few hours.

~

Saturday morning, four weeks before the wedding, Tauni, Zoey, and I mixed and baked until noon and threw in laughter for good measure. Zoey and Tauni hit it off well after only meeting once before at the engagement party a few weeks earlier. And Tauni thanked me again for inviting her over and getting her to laugh. She seemed in better spirits when she left than when she arrived.

A little after 4:00 p.m., Blake and I took Zoey out to see the location of our new house and to visit my tree.

A short way down the driveway, Blake stopped his pickup, a few feet behind where Quade and Sonny were walking. "I forgot to tell him something earlier today." Blake jumped out of his truck and strode toward Quade.

I rolled my window down and stuck my head out to greet him.

After he waved back, Blake placed his arm over Quade's shoulder. "Have you ever read the book of Hosea?"

I smiled. *I love that man. The same thing I asked him a month ago when I talked with him about forgiveness.*

He climbed into the truck and drove to our new homesite.

"Such a beautiful place for a house." Zoey gazed across the land with wide eyes.

We strolled toward the tree. I shared about my special times talking to God at a similar tree on my grandparent's farm. I told Blake and Zoey that I'd accepted Jesus as my Lord and Savior at a tree I called, "the tree of life."

"That tree looks more beautiful all the time, just like you," Blake said.

Zoey's interest piqued, and she asked several

questions about faith and God. I rejoiced that the Lord was at work in her heart.

Blake held my hand while we made our way back to his truck. "What do you think about naming our ranch? Maybe 'Conner's Ranch?'"

"If we plan to grow roses here too, we could name it 'Conner's Garden.'"

He rubbed his chin. "Your maiden name was Adams, right?"

"Yes." I stopped walking and peered at him.

After a minute, he grinned. "We could name it in memory of your parents and grandparents. What do you think about 'Adam's Garden?'"

"That's unnecessary," I rested my head on his shoulder, "but I love it."

Zoey took my hand and whispered in my ear. "He loves you so much."

"We're both blessed to be loved by the Conner men."

Blake pointed to where the crew had cleared the trees at the road. "I'll order a wrought-iron sign that says, 'Welcome to Adam's Garden' and place it over the entrance of our driveway."

I smiled. "Adam's Garden. Where visitors find a haven of rest and the tree of life."

Twenty-four

Zoey accepted my invitation to attend church with me, and Blake joined us there. Afterward, we went to lunch at Blake's house. His kitchen smelled heavenly. He smoked a chicken that was ready when we arrived. His chef came by on his day off and pulled the chicken from the smoker and prepared au gratin potatoes, a salad, and fresh steamed veggies.

I placed my hand on the back of Blake's shoulder as he warmed the food. "Are you trying to impress Zoey?"

"You are the only woman I wish to amaze." He kissed my cheek. "Have I succeeded in my quest?"

I nodded. "Zoey and I will set the table."

"Why don't you show Zoey around the house." He turned toward her. "Did you see much of it when you were here before?"

She shook her head. "Can we go upstairs?"

"We can go wherever you'd like." I took her by the hand.

We took the elevator up to the second floor and walked down the hallway past the main staircase which led to the wide-opened foyer. Zoey backtracked to the top of the stairs. "Are we planning to come down these stairs for the wedding? That would be beautiful."

"Jenny suggested it too. If you think we can do it with no challenges. I'm concerned about your belly. I'd hate for you to lose your balance and fall."

"Oh, my. But if someone escorts me down, I guess I'll be fine."

"Jim could escort you, and Carl could walk with me. What do you think?"

We agreed that would be our plan and made a few more along the way.

We peered into the bedrooms, bathrooms, theater, and recording studio. Zoey wanted to get a closer look at the studio, and I continued down the hallway to get a look at Blake's office. I'd peeked in on another occasion but didn't venture inside.

Reggie Batson's book, *Second Chances*, rested on Blake's desk. I picked it up and thumbed through the pages. Blake bought the book in Albuquerque when we were there for the healthcare conference. We'd met the author on one of our flights, and he impressed Blake.

On the dedication page, I read what Mr. Batson wrote when he signed Blake's copy. "You two make the cutest couple. I'm certain the Lord will bless your marriage. God's best to you both."

I chuckled. No wonder Blake didn't want to show this to me when he first bought it. Reggie mentioned marriage before we became a couple.

Zoey entered the office and I placed the book back on Blake's desk. "I'm ready to get back to the kitchen. I'm starving."

"Let's go." I took a few steps toward the elevator. "Want to descend the stairs for a practice? I'll be your escort."

She giggled and took my arm.

~

Later that afternoon, Zoey and I packed a few more of my things, and she spent time on a call with Andy. Afterward, we discussed more details of our weddings. We called to check in with Allison and asked how the plans were progressing. I put my phone on speaker so Zoey could listen in.

Allison said, "I ordered the roses for the tables and bouquets. Zoey requested a mixed bouquet of various colors, and Dad asked that yours remain a secret for now."

"That's not fair. Zoey got to pick hers." I pouted and wrinkled my nose.

Zoey laughed. "Keedryn made a face at you."

Allison chuckled. "Not my fault. Dad said yours are special, but he needs to tell you about the color first. He said if you don't like them, we can order what you do like."

I twisted my mouth. "Okay, I'll blame the boss man."

~

Monday, Zoey called me at the office after the mail arrived and told me the invitations came. She asked if she could open the package. I told her yes and called Jenny to let her know. She wasn't subbing that week and offered to drive to my place so she and Zoey could address envelopes and get them mailed.

Blake and I enjoyed lunch at a fancy-named burger restaurant. The name didn't improve the greasiness of the sandwich, but their fries were delicious.

"What about our wedding rings?" I dipped a fry in ketchup and gobbled it.

"I have a band that matches your ring. Do you want

me to pick out my wedding band without you or do you want to go with me?"

"I don't know why you'd need me." *Didn't need me to pick out the color of my bouquet.* "I guess you can get that on your own."

"What about a honeymoon? Do you want to go with me, or should I handle that on my own too?"

I narrowed my eyes. "Are you asking about seeing a travel agent together to plan one or the actual honeymoon?"

He smiled.

"If I were sitting next to you, I'd slap you. Of course, I'll go on the honeymoon with you."

"Should I invite Allison to join us?"

I pursed my lips and shook my head. "You'd better not." I gazed into his eyes and raised my eyebrows. "Do you have any suggestions where we should go?"

"No. I've been everywhere. We should stay home." Blake took a drink of his cola.

I jerked my head back and narrowed my eyes. "What about Europe? New Zealand? Hawaii? Or a cruise?"

He rested his elbow on the table and brought his fist to his chin. "A cruise? Leave it up to me. February is the perfect time to tour Alaska."

"You're such a tease." I sighed. "Surprise me. I have a passport from a trip Sam and I took six years ago to Canada so I'm ready unless we need immunizations."

We finished our burgers and paid the bill. Inside his car, I asked, "Have you worked out the details for the reception's food and music?"

"Got it all covered. Chef Richard is an expert, the piano player from our engagement party is coming back for the wedding music, and I secured a band for the reception."

"Great. I'm thankful it's all coming together. We'll need to pick out songs."

He pulled out into the road and stopped at a traffic light. "Oh. I thought you wanted me to do that too. We've got it covered."

I gasped and straightened. "Who's we?"

"Me and my main girl."

"Allison?"

He shook his head. "Nicki."

I opened my eyes wide. "Nicki helped you pick out songs for our wedding?"

Blake focused on the road. "She offered brilliant suggestions."

I spoke in a frustrated tone. "What songs? She's six. Anything she picks will be from Disney movies."

"Yep. We're having a Disney wedding for my queen and my princess." He chuckled. "You put me in charge, and I called on Nicki to help. We will not disappoint you."

I gaped at him. *I can't believe this. He's taking care of what food we eat, Nicki helped him with music, Allison picked out my dress, she and Jenny selected the invitations. And I just told him to surprise me with our honeymoon. What do I get to do?*

When we got back to the BCH parking lot, I followed Blake into his office suite to see how Tauni was doing. We stood near her desk, although she wasn't there.

"Has Tauni or Quade said anything about them getting back together?"

Blake rubbed his chin. "She didn't tell you?"

"Tell me what?"

"I took care of everything. They're back together. Quade's taking her to Samson's this Friday."

"*You* took care of everything?" *Unbelievable.* "What did you do?"

"I'm a master matchmaker and cannot share my secrets."

I stared at him and squinted. "The book of Hosea won again, didn't it?" I placed my hands on my hips. "You're taking credit for something I shared with you last month and the Lord shared years ago."

He grinned. "That book opened my eyes to forgiveness. I'm glad God spoke to Quade's heart as well. We both helped to get them back together."

Tauni entered the office and slung her purse across her desk. "Men."

I grimaced and eyed Blake. "Or not."

~

After work, I hurried home and found Jenny pulling out of the parking lot. She circled back around and told me that she and Zoey had finished addressing the invitations, and she was taking them to the post office. I thanked her for getting them done.

Zoey met me at the door wringing her wrist. "I haven't experienced writer's cramp like this since essays in high school."

I picked up an invitation. "They turned out fantastic, didn't they?"

Smiling, she hugged me. "I'm excited to see both of our names on them. Thank you for making this happen."

I sniffed. "What do I smell?"

"Macaroni and cheese. My homemade recipe."

"Yum." I put my arm across her shoulder and

squeezed. "Can't wait to try it. One of my favorites."

~

Wednesday, Tauni and I met for lunch. After her lunch with Quade on Monday, she wasn't in the mood to discuss their romantic life. I expected her to update me on their relationship today. I wanted her and Quade to work things out.

"Blake barked at me this morning." She pouted and crossed her arms. "He asked me to redo a letter that was fine."

"Don't take it personally. You're doing an outstanding job. He must be having an awful day."

"Did you two have a fight?"

I smiled. "Not that I remember, but we're both dealing with a lot of extra stress over the wedding plans. I'm sure it wasn't about you."

Tauni sounded uncertain of herself. "Has he told you that I'm doing an outstanding job?"

"No, but he'd tell me if you weren't."

She then told me that Quade apologized for telling her things wouldn't work out between them. He said he realized his mistake after studying his Bible and praying.

"Wonderful. But what happened Monday at lunch?"

"He told me that he was falling in love with me, but he didn't think I was marriage material."

"Whoa." I sat back. "Mixed messages. I understand your frustration. Have you spoken to him since?"

"I'm not answering his calls. Before I left the restaurant, he tried to clarify what he'd said and told me that I must have misunderstood. I don't think I did. But it's too late. He'll keep hurting me. I've endured enough of that over the years."

"Have you ever said something but knew it didn't

express your genuine feelings or what you wanted to convey?" I drew my eyebrows together and softened my tone. "Maybe you could give him another opportunity."

"I can't take the chance he'll break my heart again."

"But you may run away from God's best for your life. Can you take that risk?"

~

After our lunch, I stepped into Blake's office to find out what upset him earlier in the day and why he barked at Tauni.

I closed the door behind me and took a seat across from his desk. "A busy day? I missed not getting to say hello this morning."

He tilted his head from side to side. "I . . . I'm undecided on how to handle this situation."

"Something here at work?"

He closed his eyes and rubbed the middle of his forehead. "My greenhouse and car. I found out who vandalized them and who stole Hank's ring." He peered at me. "Cindy Walker."

I reached across his desk to touch his hand. "Oh, no."

He shook his head. "She's been arrested for the theft, but I struggle with whether I should file charges for the vandalism. She's already been through a lot with her mother's death."

I leaned back. "How awful. Will she go to jail for stealing the ring?"

"That's possible unless the judge goes easy on her."

"So sad, but vandalism and stealing are not appropriate ways to deal with sorrow or anger."

"I agree, but I understand why Cindy might hate me." He sighed and rubbed the back of his neck. "What do you think I should do?"

"Won't the insurance company file charges for what they paid to cover the repairs to your car?"

"I suppose you're right, and they'll do the same with my homeowners' policy. What do you think about me not pressing charges and let the insurance company battle it out with her?"

"That keeps you out of it, so I like the idea. But it may take years before Cindy lets this go." I clasped my hands under my chin. "Like I said before, I hope she finds peace."

Twenty-five

Mid-February

Two weeks later, and nine days before the wedding, we'd checked off everything on our to-do-list. We were ready for our grand event except for one minor item—Andy hadn't arrived. The job he'd promised to see through to completion hadn't ended on the Saturday before as planned. Now he felt certain they'd finish on Friday, and he'd be on his way to Nashville by Monday.

Zoey paced, ranted, and cried since hearing that news five days ago. Her hormones nearly drove me insane. I did my best to reassure her all would work out and Andy would arrive on time. That was one week where I found joy going into the office each day.

Vivian called me before lunch that morning and sounded frantic. "Mom took a nasty fall. We're in the ER now."

"How bad? Will she need to stay long?"

"They said she fractured her hip. They'll do surgery and she'll spend a few weeks in rehab." She sounded discouraged. "We won't make it to your wedding."

"Not a problem. I'll fly down on Saturday and spend a few days to help."

"Oh no you won't. We'll be fine. Come see us after your honeymoon."

"Okay, but if you need me, please call. And we'll help with the medical bills." We disconnected the call.

For lunch, Blake took me to his house. Chicken salad sandwiches were ready and waiting on us. Blake's chef at work. I must admit, he was a kind man and an excellent cook.

We chatted about Aunt Mary and talked about visiting her soon.

After our lunch, Blake said he had a gift for me. Not surprising, since it was Valentine's Day.

He led me to the greenhouse in his backyard. "After the repairs, this place looks brand new. Would you like to see inside?"

I grasped his arm. "I'd love to."

We entered and passed the lovely salmon colored roses he'd given me in the past. He walked me to a beautiful ivory colored rose with a soft pink center. "I only have one in bloom because of the vandalism, but these roses are for you."

I brushed my fingertip across one petal. "Beautiful. I love them." I gazed into Blake's eyes and whispered. "Thank you."

"I'm saving this one until I can give you two together."

"Why two?"

"Two roses signify mutual love and affection, and to me they show we'll be a couple forever. The ivory color represents charm, thoughtfulness, grace, and perfection."

"And ivory is the color of my bridal bouquet?"

He nodded. "Only if you want them. Your decision."

"Great. I'd like to add a few lavender or pink roses to the center of the bouquet with the ivory ones encircling them."

"If that's what you want, you've got it." He cupped his hands around my face. "You have enriched my life with your thoughtfulness and grace."

"Well, aren't you the charming one?"

He kissed my lips and embraced me. "And you, my love, are pure perfection."

~

Friday was my last day at Boden Combs Healthcare. Beth and I invited Tauni to join us for lunch at our favorite deli. Tauni and I hadn't gotten together on Wednesday, and I planned to get the details on why she'd canceled.

Beth asked me what my plans were for a job. I told her I'd wait on the Lord and walk through whichever door He opened for me. She then excused herself to the restroom.

I nudged Tauni's arm. "Well? What happened between you and Quade? Is he the reason we didn't meet Wednesday?"

She blushed and smiled. "We made up last weekend and spent a lot of time together this week."

"Everything worked out?"

She glanced at me. "I misunderstood what he said. I heard, 'I don't think.' But he said, 'Guy won't think you're marriage material.' That's his brother. I'm glad Quade didn't give up and kept pursuing me to find out why I'd gotten upset."

"Does it bother you that his brother, Guy, doesn't think you'll be good for Quade?"

She laughed. "Oh, it's not because of my past.

Quade promised to keep that information between us. No, it's because I don't like football."

I raised my eyebrows. "You must be kidding. You almost split up over football?"

She peered at me. "I think Blake kept after him to not give up on me."

"Sounds like Blake." I chuckled.

Beth returned to our booth, frowned, and wrinkled her nose at me. "I'll miss you when you're gone. Could we get together for lunch one day each week like you and Tauni?"

I grinned. "I'd love that. What about on Mondays or Fridays?"

Tauni opened her eyes wide. "No. On Wednesdays with us. I'll need all the help I can get if Quade and I continue our relationship."

~

Saturday morning, one week before our wedding, I loaded several boxes into the back of my car to take to Blake's house. A few filled with clothes for the master closet and the rest to store in the attic. Blake helped unload them and together we took them upstairs.

When there was only one more box for the attic to bring up, he suggested I stay put and wait on him to retrieve it. "Now might be a good time for you to check out Cheryl's unfinished projects down the hall if you're interested in seeing them."

"The one you showed me a month ago was beautiful. I'd love to see more."

I slipped down the attic hallway and entered her art room. I pulled back the coverings on each painting and admired the beauty of her creations. Roses, landscapes, and colorful abstracts. I unscrewed the canvas holder on a tall wooden easel and lifted a landscape to get a closer look. A notebook that looked like those Cheryl journaled in, fell to the floor. I opened to the first page and saw the date of February 14 from six years earlier. When I flipped to the last page with writing, I saw she'd written the date of March 6 at the top of the entry. The day she died.

I closed the journal, hurried down the hall, and found Blake placing my final box on top of the others we'd brought to the attic.

He straightened and looked at me. "That's the final box. I'll bring the truck by and pick up the chest you want to keep too." He cocked his head. "What's in your hand?"

"Cheryl's last journal." I handed it to Blake.

He took it from me and leaned his back against the wall. He flipped to the last page with handwriting and read aloud. "I've been asking the Lord to reveal the truth to me of what happened between Blake and Eliza. I now believe Eliza's been lying to me all along. Blake has been faithful all our years together." His voice trailed off. "And I'm sure he loves me."

That was what Blake needed to hear. To know Cheryl believed in him.

He glanced at me, smiled, and continued to read. "I've also prayed over my depression and what I must do." Blake slid down the wall and onto the floor. "I'm ready to get counseling and plan to tell Blake today." His smile faded and he rubbed his bottom lip.

I took a seat on the floor next to him and rubbed his arm.

He took a deep breath before he continued. "The only thing I hope is that he won't suggest committing me to a hospital or suicide prevention program." Blake closed his eyes for a few seconds. "I want to stay home and receive his and my family's love and support through this. I can get through anything with Blake and the Lord by my side."

He stared straight ahead and spoke in a flat tone. "My fault she died."

I held onto his arm. "Not true."

He stood. "If I'd known she wanted to ask me for help and hadn't insisted she receive inpatient treatment, she wouldn't have left upset. I'd still have my wife." He stormed out of the attic while I remained on the floor.

I'd still have my wife? Where would that leave me?

~

I left without seeing Blake. Not because I didn't want to, but because his house was huge, and I didn't know where he'd be. We both needed time to think. Although I understood why he said what he did, it hurt.

Zoey sat on my couch with her phone to her ear when I entered my condo. "Are you going to leave Monday? . . . But it's a two-day trip. That's cutting it close. . . Are you sure?" She sounded frustrated. "So, you promise to get here Wednesday?" She disconnected the call and stood. "They won't finish now until Monday. What if he doesn't make it?"

"I'm sure he'll do everything he can to get here. Wednesday is okay. We have until Friday to get the marriage licenses, and Friday evening we'll have the rehearsal. Everything will work out." I hugged and held her for a minute.

After lunch, Zoey went to her room to take a nap while I kept busy with housework. *I'd still have my wife? We're supposed to get married in a week and he wants*

Cheryl back? I can't believe this is happening. Why now?

Blake showed up at my door at 3:15 with a bouquet of orange roses in his hands. *Like that's going to fix this.* When he handed them to me, he said, "I made an insensitive comment, not thinking about how it must have sounded to you. Please accept these with my apology."

I held the bouquet in my hands and counted fifteen flowers. The correct number of roses to say, "I'm sorry." I brought them to my nose and sniffed. Without looking at him, I said in a monotone voice, "What do orange roses mean?"

He spoke above a whisper. "New beginnings."

"Oh." I handed him the bouquet. "Roses don't fix everything, Blake. I felt betrayed today. I need to feel safe and secure in your love. But I'm not sure I do now." I brought my fist up to my lips.

He placed the roses on my coffee table and hugged me. He caressed my hair and whispered affirmations in my ear. When he released me, his eyes filled with tears. He told me how much he loved me and how important I was to him.

I let out a lengthy sigh and spoke with tenderness. "You need to understand you did all you could for Cheryl. I believe that on the day of her fatal accident, she was coming home to tell you what she hadn't told you before she left that day. That she knew you were faithful to her, and she wanted your help." I took Blake's hands in mine. "And to tell you that she loved you, as I do."

~

Blake hadn't heard yet that Andy wouldn't leave until Tuesday. "What if there's another hold up and he doesn't make it in time?" Blake paced my living room.

"Now you sound like Zoey." I ambled to the kitchen. "He'll make it."

"But if he doesn't?" He followed me and sat at the table. "We won't postpone, will we? I want to get this over with."

"Over with?" I pinched the bridge of my nose and squeezed my eyes shut.

He stood and touched my shoulder. "I meant I want to get started with our 'new beginnings.'"

"Oh, right." I shook my head. "We'll get married, even if he doesn't make it. Zoey will have to understand."

"Understand what?" Zoey wiped her hand across her eyes. "Oh, no. You talked to Andy and he won't be here by Friday?" She brought both hands to her cheeks.

I give up. I lifted my hands. "Stop now. He'll be here." I softened my tone. "But if he isn't, Blake and I plan to get married a week from today."

She trudged to the sofa and sat. "I'll expect you to get married if we do or not. Wouldn't want you to wait when you're this close."

I knelt next to her and held her hand. "The three of us will pray and trust God that Andy will arrive on time." *Please, God? Zoey will be heartbroken if he doesn't make it.*

Twenty-six

Zoey received a call from Andy on Wednesday during our breakfast. "You're where? . . . Oklahoma City? How far away is that?" Her voice rose in intensity and volume. "How many hours? . . . Tomorrow? Andy?" She shoved her phone into her pocket and sniffled. "My car broke down. He's getting it fixed."

My face brightened. "And he'll be here tomorrow?"

"No. He has to wait on the parts to get there. He won't be able to leave until sometime tomorrow." She wiped her tears. "He said it's almost 700 miles to Nashville."

Oh, no. He may not arrive on time. With more confidence than I felt, I said, "If he gets here by 3:30 p.m. on Friday we'll be okay. We can hurry over to the county clerk's office and get our licenses." I patted her hand. "Take a deep breath."

"Can we pray together again?"

I nodded, closed my eyes, and thanked the Lord for working in Zoey's heart before I prayed out loud.

After our prayer, I suggested she put her feet up, and I called Blake to fill him in. He asked how Zoey was coping.

"She'll make it, but I hope her stress doesn't cause the baby anxiety too. I keep praying for him or her."

"I'll call Andy and see how he's doing. He could leave the car there and fly here if it looks like they can't get the part he needs. We can pick up the car after our honeymoon."

"Is our destination a surprise?"

"That's what you said you wanted." He chuckled.

"But how will I know what to pack?"

"If you pack the wrong things, I'll buy you a new wardrobe."

I giggled. "Maybe I won't pack anything. I like the sound of new clothes."

~

After an uneventful Wednesday afternoon and evening and minimal distractions on Thursday, we spent most of Friday getting Blake's foyer, great room, and the full downstairs ready for the wedding. Blake, Jim, and Carl moved furniture out of the great room to provide more room for tables. Jenny, Allison, Zoey, and I helped with the decorations. Zoey was a mess at 2:00 p.m. when Andy hadn't arrived. I became antsy at 2:30, and Blake kept his cool until 3:00. He and Zoey both called Andy several times, but he didn't answer.

I slipped around the corner and into the laundry room to find a quiet place to pray. Blake and I planned to leave at 3:30 to drive to Franklin for our marriage license whether Andy arrived or not. But I could only imagine what that would do to Zoey. Depending on traffic, the drive could take as long as thirty minutes and their office closed at 4:30.

At 3:22, Andy zipped into the driveway. Zoey, Blake, and I rushed outside and after a quick round of hugs, the four of us climbed into Blake's Infiniti and headed south to the County Clerk's office. Andy explained that he didn't answer our calls because the distractions would slow him down.

When we arrived at the building, we were already ten minutes behind schedule because of an accident on I-65. We followed the signs to the correct counter to apply for marriage licenses. We fretted with only twenty-five minutes to get to the front of the line.

Two women worked the windows for the licenses, and four couples stood in front of us. We needed the process for getting a license to not take longer than ten minutes per couple.

Giggles bubbled up inside of me. Once I get started, it's hard to stop. I stifled them and put on a serious face. The four of us chatted for several minutes, which helped to pass the time. But we got concerned we wouldn't make it to the front before they closed. At 4:20 with one couple in front of us, Blake pulled out his cash.

"What are you doing?" My eyes grew wide.

"I may need to offer a bribe for someone to stay past closing. I'm checking to see how much cash I have."

"A bribe? Put your money away. Prayer works, bud."

Andy snickered. "You call him bud?"

"No. That's who he is at this moment." I grinned.

"You must have as many names for Dad as Allison does for me."

"Stick with me, kid. You ain't heard nothin' yet."

I nudged Blake's elbow and winked. "Hey, big guy. We're in line for a marriage license. Bet you faced a few doubts about that ever happening."

"Behave yourself." Blake rolled his eyes.

"Do I embarrass you?"

Zoey laughed at us just before she and Andy approached one of the clerks. The couple at the other window turned and rushed away after being at the counter for only a few minutes. The woman mumbled something about the man needing to memorize his social security number.

"Next." The clerk glanced at Blake and me. The clock on the wall behind her read 4:28.

I grabbed Blake's hand and pulled him forward. "We want to apply for a marriage license."

"The young couple at the next window took the last one for today." She smiled for a moment. "Just kidding."

I chuckled and looked at Blake. "Wow. I thought we might need to fly to Vegas tonight."

Blake grimaced and crossed his arms. "Have you been drinking today?"

"Blake Conner." I shoved him in a playful way. "You know I don't drink."

"I've never seen you like this."

"I've never gotten a marriage license with you before now."

The lady behind the counter sneered. "Sir, if she's always this abusive, perhaps you should reconsider."

Blake put on the country charm, a twangy, southern drawl. "Ma'am. I've reconsidered several times since I gave her the ring."

She gave me a sideways glance. "How long have you been engaged?"

Blake shook his head and wrinkled his nose. "Seven long weeks."

The woman leaned toward Blake and attempted to speak in a whisper. "If she annoys you now, why marry her?"

Blake shrugged. "She's a splendid cook." How he kept a straight face, I'll never know.

Poor Zoey. We must have been a distraction. She laughed again and held her belly.

I tried to keep my giggles in check but failed and snatched a tissue from my purse.

We hurried through the application process. I dropped my ID on the floor. Twice. When I stooped to pick it up the second time, Blake stepped on it. An accident, he said. The grin on his face told me otherwise. He paid our fee and the kid's fee.

I held the paperwork and waved it over my head. "We have a license."

The lady behind the counter scrunched her face. "Ma'am. You know you're not married? An official qualified to perform the ceremony must sign the license." She was serious.

I wiped the silly smile off my face. "Yes. Thank you. We'll have a ceremony and have this signed." I burst into laughter once we made it outside.

~

We rushed back to Blake's house to run through our rehearsal with Manuel and the rest of the family. We practiced our walk down the staircase and the songs. All but Blake's. He said his song was a surprise. Manuel and his wife, Susie, stayed afterward and joined us for dinner.

Blake kept a silly grin on his face all evening. He called me over to him when only close family members remained and while they were all busy chatting. "I have something for you."

I smiled back at him. He was almost as giddy as me when we got our marriage license earlier.

"Your pet name. I came up with one all on my own. No Google involved."

I stared at him and waited for the big-name revelation.

"Are you ready?"

I nodded and giggled.

"Kiwi."

"Like the fruit?" *That's kind of cute.* "So, I'm sweet and remind you of a healthy treat?"

His smile faded and he narrowed his eyes. "Fruit? Sure. Does that mean you like it?"

"I thought I did. But now I'm not convinced that's why you picked this name. Why did you choose kiwi?"

He glanced at his feet. "When I polished my shoes this morning, I was thinking of you."

I took a step back and frowned. My voice rose in volume. "You named me after your shoe polish?" I shook my head and muttered. "I guess I'm just here to make you look good."

He took hold of my arms and gazed into my eyes. "The K I in Kiwi has the same sound as K E E in Keedryn, and they are the first two letters in the word 'kind.'" He beamed. "And the W I is pronounced 'we' as in us—a couple forever. That's why it's the perfect name for you."

I relaxed and hugged his neck. "I love it. Superb job."

"What do you plan to call me?" He took a step back and peered at me.

"What about nugget?"

"I remind you of a bite-size piece of chicken?"

I cupped his cheek in my palm. "You are a treasure—a nugget of great value to me."

~

Allison and Jenny joined Zoey and me at my place that night for a sleepover. We made plans to leave for Blake's at 10:00 a.m. and use the in-law quarters until our ceremony at 1:30 p.m.

While the ladies chatted in the living room, I stood in my kitchen with my stomach in knots. I rubbed my arms, looked around me, and felt a sudden urge to be alone. I slipped away to my room and sat on my bed. My chest tightened. *What am I doing? Getting married tomorrow? Am I ready for this?*

I sighed. "Sam, I love and miss you. We were perfect for each other. I'll never forget you, but I've found someone who will love and care for me. I'm sure that's what you would have wanted, but I'm a little scared."

Twenty-seven

The next morning, after our sleepover and an evening of chatter and giggles, Jenny, Allison, Zoey, and I left for Blake's. I'd packed for a ten-day honeymoon and strolled to Jenny's car.

We waved to Zoey and Allison when they honked their horn and drove away.

Jenny placed my suitcases in her trunk, and I climbed into the front passenger seat. I stared through the windshield and became concerned about Roxie. Jenny patted my leg and assured me that she and Nicki would take excellent care of my cat until I returned home.

I picked at my fingernails. "What if Blake thinks I'm a terrible wife? For a while, he thought I was a terrible assistant."

Jenny chuckled. "Mom. You sound like a crazy woman. Stop." She shook her head. "You will be a wonderful wife. He only acted like you were a poor assistant. You know that. Now take a deep breath and relax."

"You don't have to laugh at me. I'm sleep deprived. I've lain awake the past few nights. Then I wake up after only a little sleep and can't remember what kept me awake." I peered at my ring. "Your dad and I molded together as one. Blake seems harder to please." I turned toward the passenger window. "I'm terrified. Do you suppose I jumped into this without thinking it through?" I didn't want Jenny to see my eyes.

"Only wedding jitters. You're perfect for each other." After she pulled into Blake's driveway and parked, she grasped my hands and offered a sweet prayer for the wedding, reception, and marriage.

We exited the car and hurried inside. Jenny's prayer helped to calm my nerves. Peace warmed my heart and quieted my mind.

~

We made ourselves at home in the in-law quarters, which was the size of my condo. After we hung our dresses in the bedroom closet, we took our seats around the table in the kitchen. This area opened to the living room and included a sofa and two recliners.

I sat with my back to the window that overlooked the front yard and felt blessed for the beautiful younger women God placed in my life.

At 11:30, we put on our makeup and curled our hair. When we finished, Jenny and Allison left to inspect the food that Blake's chef prepared.

Jenny returned with finger foods, and Allison carried in a plate filled with desserts.

"I can't eat anything." I clutched my middle with both hands. "Too excited."

"Me either." Zoey squirmed. "I'm too nervous."

Jenny placed her hands on her hips. "You both must eat. Neither of you ate much breakfast. Please?"

"More important for me to laugh." I eyed Allison and Jenny. "Who has a funny story to share? Maybe something that happened at one of your weddings."

Allison joined Zoey and me at the table. "I have one.

When I got married, Dad walked me down the aisle. We got to the front, and he battled second thoughts about letting go of his baby girl. The preacher said, 'Who gives this woman to be married to this man?' With tears in his eyes, Dad said, 'Her mother and I.' Then he got in Jim's face. 'If you break her heart, I'll search for you, and I *will* find you.'"

I cringed. "How did Jim react?"

"He stared at me with fear in his eyes because he knew wealth brings power. He stammered, 'Sir. You have my word. I will treasure her like gold. I will love her always and be a wonderful husband to her.' But he whispered in my ear, 'Can we move to Canada or someplace farther away? He frightens me.'"

"Now that sounds like Jim." I chuckled.

Someone knocked on the door. "Guests arriving." Jim brought the news.

"Zoey and I should put on our dresses." I stood and giggled. "Let's go." I motioned for her to follow me. "Could someone help me with my zipper?" I glanced at Jenny. "Are my hair and makeup okay?"

She wrapped her arm across my shoulder. "You're stunning. And you seem more relaxed than you did when we first arrived."

I opened my eyes wide. "That's because the Lord has filled me with His peace."

"Great. I'm glad our time of prayer in the car helped."

We all hurried into the bedroom.

Jenny rushed to the closet. "I love Mom's dress. Allison, you did a splendid job picking this out. I love the lavender with the deep purple, and Mom's bouquet will make it more gorgeous."

Allison pulled Zoey's dress out of the closet and handed it to her. "Your dress is lovely too. The light blue highlights your eyes." She kissed her new sister-in-law on the cheek. "You're beautiful."

Zoey blushed.

I took Jenny by the arm and spoke in a whisper. "Have you tried on your dress? You're getting a little pudgy."

She glared at me. "Only a little baby bump. I assure you I can fit into my dress."

My daughter appeared offended. I hugged her and apologized.

Allison and Jenny wore matching dresses, but in different colors. Pale green and pink. Jenny's dress was a little tight, but I didn't dare mention it again.

Zoey laughed. "We'll look like Easter eggs lined across the front. Green, blue, purple, and pink."

We laughed along with her. She had become a part of our new family.

I put my arm around her shoulders and squeezed. "Ladies. I'd like to pray for us. For our weddings today and for our matrons of honor."

We joined hands in a circle and talked to God. I didn't plan for others to pray. Just happened. I started, and Jenny and Allison followed. I opened my mouth to close, so Zoey didn't feel obligated and think she needed to say anything. But a quiet voice spoke next to me.

"God. This is Zoey. You don't know me, but You know my new family. Thank you for giving them to me."

"We all said, 'Amen.'"

I hugged Zoey. "He knows you well. And He loves you more than you can imagine."

~

A few minutes after 1:00, the four of us made our way upstairs with our bouquets and stood back from the main stairway, so no one would see us. Voices from below drifted upward past us.

"Zoey? Are you ready?" I touched her elbow.

She gnawed on her bottom lip. "Please ask God to help me with my song."

"I will. You'll do great."

After several minutes, the chatter downstairs stopped. Our pianist played Nicki's favorite song from the Disney movie, *Frozen*.

I inched my way closer to the banister that overlooked the foyer below and whispered to Zoey. "We can peek from here without being seen." We hid behind a column and took turns poking our heads out.

Nicki entered the foyer from the kitchen hallway. She skipped and whirled down the aisle, tossing various colors of rose petals here and there. Allison and Jenny descended the stairs and danced and twirled to the music like Nicki. Silly girls.

"We didn't practice that, but they're adorable." I ducked out of the way. "I've got to hide. Jim will come up to escort you soon. I suggest that you move to the top of the stairs now."

The top of his head came into view. I scurried around the corner. When he told Zoey how stunning she looked, I smiled.

I wanted to see Andy's expression when he saw his beautiful bride, but I couldn't see him from where I hid, which disappointed me.

His booming voice sang a Disney classic from *Aladdin*, followed by the quieter, but lovely voice of Zoey as she joined the duet and sang to her groom.

The music stopped, Carl bounded up the stairs, and I glided toward him.

~

I inhaled a long, deep breath and released it slowly. If someone had told me five months earlier that I'd marry Blake Conner, I would have laughed in their face. But here I am. About to marry the man who almost caused me to quit my job because of his arrogance, condescending attitude, and short temper. In a few moments, I will become Mrs. Blake Conner. Only God could accomplish that.

"Sorry I'm a little late. I had to get Nicki seated." Carl's eyes glowed. "Are you ready?"

"I believe so." I took his elbow, and he led me to the top of the stairway. My stomach fluttered. The song from below sounded familiar, but I couldn't place it. I expected a song from a Disney animated feature, but I detected a country feel. When Blake's baritone voice rang out, I wrinkled my forehead and stared at Carl with my mouth opened.

He grinned. "Rascal Flatts. They sang it in a Disney teen movie about ten years ago."

We made our way down the stairs. My man impressed me by singing a beautiful love song. Endearing. Blake and the song.

I reached Blake, gave my rose bouquet to Jenny, and took his hands in mine. When he finished the song, I couldn't help myself. I moved in for a kiss.

Manuel moved closer. "No. Wait. You can't do that, Keedryn. I haven't pronounced you husband and wife."

Several guests laughed. I turned toward them and hid my face in my hands to pretend embarrassment.

Manuel frowned, shook his head, and chuckled.

"Blake and Andy hold two roles here today. They're both grooms and each other's best man. I'll turn the ceremony over to them now to share a special moment with you."

Blake moved in front of Andy and Zoey, placed his hands on their shoulders, and spoke a sweet blessing over their marriage and family. He encouraged them to put God first, each other second, and family third.

Andy reached into a small container he'd placed nearby and brought out two ivory roses. He stepped in front of Blake and me and handed the first rose to Blake. "Dad, your rose symbolizes your love and affection toward Keedryn and your lifelong commitment to her."

After handing me the second rose, he said, "Keedryn, your rose represents the many gifts you've given my dad and your future gifts. You've brought joy to his heart, peace to his soul, and love again to his life. You're perfect for him." He smiled at us both. "Please exchange roses."

I gave Blake my rose and he gave me his.

Andy embraced us in a group hug. "I hope you enjoy many years of celebrating life together."

Manuel then performed the traditional vows but gave us the opportunity to add our own. Andy and Zoey shared first.

"Zoey. The first time I saw you, I thought you were the most beautiful girl I'd ever seen. After I met you, I knew that was true. You are sweet, caring, and understanding. Qualities I desire in the person I'm to spend my life with. Thank you for loving me."

"Andy. You are the man of my dreams. I've always wondered what it would be like to be loved, cared for, and respected. You've shown me those things and much more. Thank you for being my friend and my genuine love."

Manuel nodded at me to say my vows.

"Blake. I fought. The Lord won. I believed I was working for you to share God's love. I never expected to share my love with you too. God designed a plan I never envisioned. We've encountered struggles, heartache too. But I can't imagine anyone I'd rather spend my remaining years with than you."

"Keedryn. Not only did the Lord win. I won too." He peeked at his notes. "I never expected to fall in love again. You shared God's love with me and showed me His acceptance and forgiveness in tangible ways. I promise to love and cherish you for the rest of my life."

After Andy and Zoey exchanged gold wedding bands, Manuel moved in front of us. I glanced at Blake and he beamed. I beamed back.

Andy handed Blake the matching band to my engagement ring, and he placed it on my finger. My heart raced and goosebumps covered my arms. *This is really happening.* Jenny nudged my elbow and offered me the wedding band for Blake. I looked from her to my new husband with joy in my heart, and we completed the ceremony.

Blake didn't wait for Manuel to say, "You may kiss your bride." He kissed me and shouted. "Thank you, Lord."

The guests chuckled. Manuel shook his head and shrugged.

Andy gazed at Zoey, took her face in his hands, and brushed his lips over hers.

"Appears they didn't need me here today," Manuel said. "But with great pleasure I introduce to you, Mr. and Mrs. Andrew Conner and Mr. and Mrs. Blake Conner."

Epilogue

Late October

Blake and I honeymooned in Hawaii—on Kauai. My first trip to Hawaii and excited to spend time there. Any island would have thrilled me. But he'd been to a few of them with Cheryl and wanted us to experience something special together. I can't wait to visit the islands again.

We returned home on March 3 in time to welcome our new granddaughter, Cheryl Rose Conner, on March 6. She came into this world on the anniversary of her grandmother's passing. Andy and Zoey are doting parents, but I wish now that we'd asked them to move into the in-law quarters in Blake's mansion before our new house was ready. I would have loved to get my hands on her every day. Her giggles brighten my life.

Aunt Mary recovered from her hip surgery well. While she was in rehab, Blake and I spent a week in Florida getting Vivian moved into a much nicer place nearby. Their new home of 1,400 square feet included a small community duck pond outside their back door. After my aunt came home, Blake flew back to Nashville, and I spent another week to help with her care and appreciated quality time with her and Vivian. I also enjoyed feeding the ducks.

Back home, I wrestled with finding a job. At first, Blake suggested I not work at all. But one day soon after, he told me at dinner he knew the perfect position for me. He requested my help with the musicians he assists. After a few months of training and working with him, I now work from home and decide who receives monetary gifts from his uncle's estate. I love the people I meet and find great satisfaction in helping such talented men and women.

Wes left BCH in early May. We were surprised when we learned that he and Robin had dated since February until BCH uncovered their secret relationship. That discovery resulted in their terminations for violating company policy. I ran into Robin at the mall last month and she told me they are getting married in November. I'm happy for them both.

On July 15, we welcomed Nicki's baby brother into our family. Charles William Monroe must be the handsomest baby boy ever born. My sweet Jenny named her son after my grandfather, Charles, and my dad, William. They call him Charlie, and I am thankful she allows us to babysit him and Nicki often.

Later in July, Tauni's dream came true. She and Quade became engaged. They haven't set a date, but she radiates joy every time we get together. I'm excited for her and feel certain they'll make it with God's blessings.

We moved into our new home on the ranch in late September. I sit on the back deck often staring at the cattle, rolling hills, and my favorite tree. My preferred room inside is the sunroom. Roxie and I spend much time there. Blake and I spend our evenings out on the veranda when the weather's nice and on the weekends, we stroll along the stream holding hands. We sometimes entertain Tim, Nicki, Cheryl, and Charlie. Grandchildren—they bless my heart.

Blake and I hope to take a trip in the spring to Italy to visit his sister in Rome. God has brought Blake and me through so much by giving us not only love for one another, but compassion for others too. Besides Blake's transformation, we've seen God work in Tauni's life, Aunt Mary, Andy, Zoey, and Quade. We believe God will work a miracle in Lydia's heart, too, and bring reconciliation between her and Blake.

That's our prayer. And we know our Lord restores relationships and blesses those who love and serve Him.

A Note from LuAnn

Dear Reader,

Thank you for reading *Charm and Perfection,* Book 3 in my *Love Comes Again* series. If you enjoyed Blake and Keedryn's story, please leave a review to help other readers discover it.

Other books in the *Love Comes Again* series include, *Only A Glimpse,* and *Let Him Go.* Please check them out here: https://www.amazon.com/gp/product/B089SRJ4B4.

To be notified when future books are released, please sign up for my blog and e-newsletter at www.luannkedwards.com or follow me on Amazon or BookBub.

Let's connect! I'd love to hear from you!
Amazon author page:
www.amazon.com/author/luannkedwards
BookBub: https://www.bookbub.com/profile/luann-k-edwards
Goodreads: https://www.goodreads.com/luannkedwards
Facebook: https://www.facebook.com/luannkedwards

Twitter: https://twitter.com/LuAnnKEdwards1

Thank you, and God bless!

LuAnn

Acknowledgements

I'm so grateful to my Lord and Savior for the continuing story of hope He birthed within my heart for the *Love Comes Again* series.

To my husband and family who love, support, and encourage me in my writing, thank you.

Much gratitude to the real Keedryn, Kedren Scales, for sharing your story on how you acquired the name, Kiwi, from the shoe polish, and for allowing me to share your nickname with my readers.

I appreciate each beta reader who gave of their time and shared their ideas with me—Ellie, Judi, Kim, Kiran, and Leah.

A big thank you to John, a former detective with the Albuquerque Police Department. I hope I didn't stray too far from the information you gave me.

And I can't forget those who offered feedback to my Facebook page, job-related survey questions. I incorporated several of your responses in *Charm and Perfection*. Cheers to Charlene, Cindy, Debbie, Emily,

Erica, Faye, Gerry, J.D., Jenny, Kathleen, Kenn, Lissa, and Mimi.

Thanks to Larry J. Leech II for your thorough critique, assistance, and as the story's final pair of eyes before I sent it to the publisher.

Finally, I'm grateful to Winged Publications, Forget Me Not Romances for the opportunity to publish my debut series.

LuAnn writes Christian contemporary romance for women who enjoy a wholesome love story that inspires faith and hope. She holds a bachelor's degree from Lee University in Cleveland, Tennessee. LuAnn is a member of American Christian Fiction Writers and has attended several writers' conferences. She grew up in Ohio, lived in Tennessee for many years, and currently resides in New Mexico with her husband of forty-five years. LuAnn adores her children, grandchildren, puggle Pebbles, and cat Paka. A former mathematics teacher and administrative professional, she enjoys reading, hiking, traveling, and spending time with her family. You may find her online at www.luannkedwards.com to learn more about her *Love Comes Again* series.